KU-639-716

Contents

Bruce Carter

THE CHILDREN WHO STAYED BEHIND

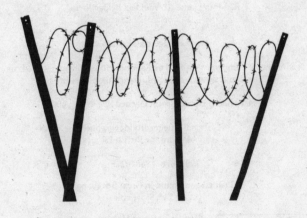

VINTAGE BOOKS
London

Published by Vintage 2015

2 4 6 8 10 9 7 5 3 1

First published in Great Britain as *The Kidnapping of Kensington* in 1958
by Hamish Hamilton

Vintage
Random House, 20 Vauxhall Bridge Road,
London SW1V 2SA

www.vintage-classics.info

Addresses for companies within The Random House Group Limited can
be found at: www.randomhouse.co.uk/offices.htm

The Random House Group Limited Reg. No. 954009

A CIP catalogue record for this book
is available from the British Library

ISBN 9781784870225

Printed and bound in Great Britain by
Clays Ltd, St Ives plc

Penguin Random House is committed to a
sustainable future for our business, our readers
and our planet. This book is made from Forest
Stewardship Council® certified paper.

To Sarah with love

1

Kensington is Threatened

GILLIAN darted round the corner, ran a few yards up the alley and flattened herself against the brick wall, holding the white rabbit tight against her. They were both so frightened that it was hard to tell whose heart was beating the faster, hers or the rabbit's. But if the danger was a mysterious, unknown one to the rabbit, to Gillian it was all too real and familiar.

The sound of running footsteps and raucous shouts from the road grew louder. Gillian could recognize Arthur's voice. He was the biggest of the Foulsham boys, a wild, ginger-haired terror, only fourteen but getting on for six feet tall. 'Tally-ho!' he was shouting ridiculously, 'we're hot on the trail . . .'

Gillian tucked the white rabbit deep into the crook of her arm and held her breath as the Foulshams went charging by barely ten feet away – eight of them with the big Arthur in the lead, the smallest Foulsham, Simon, following as well as he could at the rear. He was only five, his high-pitched hunting cry and arm-waving a mockery of his eldest brother's.

'Pack of idiots!' Gillian called after them, not too loudly. All noise and bluster they were, without an ounce of sense between them, in spite of their bearded giant of a father who was supposed to be such a genius.

'It's all right now,' Gillian went on in the soft voice she always used when talking to her animals, though it was not easy to talk in a calming manner when you were panting so hard. She stroked back the rabbit's long whiskers and let them spring up again one by one, touched her nose against the warm button of the rabbit's nose, and stared for a moment into the blank, unwavering pink eyes. 'You are very beautiful – and you are mine, Kensington,' Gillian said slowly. 'And now we'll go home.'

Gillian Hartford's home was half a mile farther along the Brighton sea front, in Lewes Crescent, Kemp Town. She would have been safer from the Foulsham children if she had followed the maze of alleys and side streets. 'But I don't think we'll see any more of that silly lot,' she said reassuringly to Kensington, 'and the sea air will do you good after all that worry.'

So Gillian walked boldly out of the sheltering alley, crossed the wide Marine Parade and set off for home along the pavement.

Beyond the Madeira Drive far below her, beyond the steel tracks of Volk's Electric Railway and the tumbling banks of piled-up pebbles, the sea shimmered like silver paper beneath party candles. Far out on the horizon the eight grey smudges of a destroyer flotilla were travelling east, grey smoke streaming behind. They had been there at breakfast time, too, 'shielding our shores from the Hun' as Gillian's father had said only half as a joke.

When Gillian paused to consider it (and she both paused and considered only rarely) she thought she would be interested to see what would happen when the Germans came. Everyone was always talking about them, and about how they were going to invade England at any minute, and after she had learnt that they were human beings and not something from outer space, she was curious to see what they looked like, too.

'It'll be fun when we're invaded, won't it?' she had suggested to Drake in the bathroom that morning. But her elder brother had not bothered even to reply, only leaving the room silently, shaking his head in despair at Gillian's flippancy.

Gillian loved this part of Brighton front, where she had lived for all her twelve and a half years, and she paused for a moment before crossing back over the road to Lewes Crescent. With Kensington's front paws resting lightly on the promenade railings, she pointed out the Palace Pier, with its minarets and cupolas and domed fun-fair halls, stretching far out into the sea; and the West Pier beyond; and the Banjo Groyne, the Black Rock swimming pool, the cliffs rising away to the east towards Rottingdean.

'It's usually full of people in the summer,' she explained, 'without all this barbed wire and these concrete things to keep the Germans away. Now no one's allowed to come to Brighton except soldiers, and you can't go on the piers – can't even go on the beach because there's a barbed wire barrier from one end to the other, and anyway you'd be blown up by mines. Not that you'd care much for the sea.'

She tucked Kensington back into the crook of her arm and turned away from the sea. 'And you'll like the garden all right. I hope you get on with Rosemary – she's a grey, quite as beautiful as you, but in a different way.'

There was no one to be seen for the whole length of the Marine Parade. The broad road had an unkempt air about it, as though no one had bothered with it for months. An old newspaper bowled and flapped its way along the gutter, and in the middle of the road there lay an empty ammunition box that had been there a week before. Gillian waited for a khaki-coloured armoured car to hum past, its tyres whistling on the tarmac, and then stepped off the kerb.

She was half-way across when she heard the sudden cry, 'There she is!'; and at once the Foulshams, still led by the hefty Arthur, poured out of the bushes in the gardens of Lewes Crescent and headed straight for her.

Gillian paused in the middle of the road, uncertain what to do, uncertain whether she had time to dash up the crescent to the front door of her house before the Foulshams cut her off. She decided she would have to retreat, duck down into the winding zigzag paths that led steeply through the shrubberies from the Marine Parade towards the sea. There she might stand a chance of throwing them off.

It was difficult running fast with Kensington, but the mere fact of carrying the precious new white rabbit made it more than ever desperately important to evade her pursuers. There was no telling what the rough, wild Foulshams might do if they were to get their hands on Kensington.

Gillian tore down the narrow path, the tamarisk and euonymous shrubs closing comfortingly about her, while Arthur's ridiculous cries of 'Tally-ho!' sounded from the road above. That great awkward lump of a boy – oh, if only Drake would suddenly appear from around the next corner! Drake would handle Arthur and all the other screaming, foolish Foulshams as he handled any crisis now, with calm, firm authority. Last time she had been caught out in the open by the Foulshams, Drake had appeared on the scene and sent them slinking back to their house, all without touching a hair of their heads. But the time before Gillian had come home with her face scratched from the bramble bush she had been hung in, upside down, by four of the biggest of them.

She darted round a sharp corner and managed to stop only just in time. Barring her way was a concrete gunpost surrounded by barbed wire. Pointing out to sea over the top of it was the grey barrel of a heavy machine-gun.

'Oh bother!' Gillian exclaimed crossly. The war whoops were coming nearer, and she was trapped. Tucking Kensington carefully into her arms, she was starting to burrow her way into the thick bushes when a voice suddenly called out, 'Hey, missy, where d'you think you're off to?'

Gillian paused for a moment, her head deep in the sweet-smelling foliage, then backed out slowly and without dignity, and stood up with her short brown hair full of twigs. A burly soldier wearing a tin hat was looking down at her over the top of the gunpost, with a broad grin on his face.

Before she had time to answer, she heard the Foulshams rounding the last corner, and saw from the sudden change of expression on the soldier's face that they had appeared in view.

'There she is – grab her!' Arthur, dressed as usual in a dirty white roll-neck sweater, was still in the lead, though holding back now to allow his younger brothers and sisters to make the capture.

Gillian braced herself against the hard concrete of the gunpost. The last time she had been caught she had left half a dozen of them with bruised faces and torn clothes and had made Arthur's nose bleed. But what could she do now with Kensington in her arms? If the worst came to the worst, she would have to let the rabbit go; on no account would she risk her being injured. Jeremy Foulsham was barely six feet away, a grin of triumph on his squat, freckled face, arms reaching out for her, when Gillian heard the soldier's voice booming out above her head.

'Keep back, you filthy cowards,' he shouted. 'Lay off all of you, or I'll break your necks one by one.' It was as if an invisible lock gate had slammed shut just in front of Gillian as the streaming torrent of Foulshams halted in their tracks.

She glanced up and saw, towering above her, the figure of the soldier standing on the top of the concrete

'What d'you think you're up to? . . .'

gunpost now, his hands on his hips. Slung over his shoulder was a tommy-gun, rifle bullets sparkled in his webbing belt, a long knife lay in its sheath over his right hip. It was not surprising that the Foulshams had skidded to a halt.

'What d'you think you're up to – eight of you against a helpless girl? Enough to make you sick, it is.' The soldier was very angry. 'And didn't you see the notice up top? "Danger Mines" it says. Place is thick with 'em. Blow the lot of you to pieces one of 'em would – not that that'd be any loss, only I'd have to sweep up the bits.'

There was sudden silence, broken only by the distant sound of another armoured car driving past on the road, and, above Gillian's head, the angry breathing of the soldier.

'Now clear off, d'you hear?' the soldier ordered.

'But, please sir, she's got our rabbit.'

Gillian spun round at the words of accusation, which came from the eldest Foulsham girl, Eleanor, a plumpish thirteen-year-old with long red hair trailing everywhere. All the Foulshams – all eight of them – had red hair of varying shades from bright new carrot to deep rust. 'That's not true,' Gillian snapped. 'I've just bought her in the market for three and six. You've never had a rabbit in your life.'

9

'I'll tell you one thing, young lady,' the soldier said, addressing Eleanor. 'I wouldn't trust you alone with me old Granny – you'd slip the rings off her fingers when she wasn't looking and sell 'em.' He jumped down with a crash from his army boots on to the path and strode towards the Foulshams, who backed away like a crowd before a raging bull. 'Now scram – d'you hear me?'

Gillian followed his steel-studded boots that went crunch-crunch purposefully up the path in pursuit of the Foulshams until they reached the Marine Parade again. There they walked hurriedly away, a silent loose bunch of dirty sweaters and slacks and shorts and mud-stained gym shoes, eight red heads retreating towards their house on the other side of Lewes Crescent.

The soldier did not say a word until they had rounded the corner and were out of sight beyond some trees; then he turned and looked down at Gillian. 'Huh!' he snorted in infinite disgust, 'there goes a scabby bunch of lice. Dunno what the world's coming to, that I don't. Where do you live, missy?'

Gillian pointed at the houses on the west side of the wide, gracious Regency terrace. 'One of those,' she said. 'I'll be all right now. Thanks very much.'

The soldier stood awkwardly, as if he did not know what to say next. 'Well . . .' and he hitched the tommy-gun more firmly on to his shoulder. 'Better be back to

my post, I suppose – just in case the Huns show up.'
He dropped a brown, gnarled hand, the biggest hand
Gillian had ever seen, gently down on to Kensington's
white head, and gave her a quick stroke. 'Pretty thing,
eh?' he said, with a little laugh, and strode off.

It was not that Gillian was ungrateful for what he had
done. Indeed she had become very fond of the soldier.
But, as she hurried across the road towards her house,
she did feel as if she had cheated. It had not been quite
fair, somehow. . . .

Many of the houses in Lewes Crescent were shut up,
with boards nailed over the windows. Most of the people
in Brighton had already left, evacuated to safer areas in
case the Germans came. Gillian and her brothers were
due to leave the day after tomorrow, too, to stay with an
uncle in Leicestershire. They would have left sooner only
their father was a doctor and had been asked to stay as
long as possible.

If Gillian had considered the matter at all, she would
have been worried at the idea of leaving her home; but
after hearing that she would be allowed to take her
animals with her, she had thought little about the matter.
Gillian lived her life as it came, rarely thinking about the
past or the future, which made her appear (especially to
her school teachers) as thoughtless and careless; which

was not true. She was not at all clever, but she was not lazy-minded. It was simply that she was quite incapable of interesting herself in things until they happened. Her father said she just bounced her way through life like an animal, and this was much nearer to the truth. Gillian shooting out of her front door or through the gates of her school was very like one of her rabbits when they were released from their cage to enjoy the freedom of the garden, racing wildly up and down, up and down, bucking and making gay little meaningless leaps in the air.

Gillian Hartford was probably the last unworried person left in Brighton. Everybody else, even her younger brother Sammy, seemed obsessed by the threat of the Germans sailing across the Channel to invade England now that they had conquered France. The only effect it had had on Gillian was to deprive her of most of her friends at school (there were only twelve children left now) – and, that afternoon, to save her from the foolish Foulshams.

Of course she noticed that there were very few people except soldiers to be seen in the streets now, that the sea front was a mass of barbed-wire entanglements and gun positions, and that most of the shops were closed. But she accepted all these things as she accepted the sudden rush of the holiday-makers who usually poured into the town in August; or as one of her rabbits accepted a new cage to live in.

The name Adelaide House was set into the glass above the double front door, which badly needed a coat of paint. Beside it were the two wide sash windows of the drawing-room, which could be opened up to join with the dining-room beyond. Below, deeply worn steps led down to the basement; above were two more floors, and the attic with little windows let into the steeply sloping roof. It was a generous, lovely house, similar to its neighbours in the gently curving crescent, but not just one in a row of identical houses as they built them now. It was a warm and welcoming house, in spite of its shabbiness. Her father said it was the sea air that made the paint chip off and the stonework lose its clean white surface so quickly.

Gillian ran up the wide steps leading to the front door, and saw that it was already open for her, her mother standing on the mat in her apron.

'Thank goodness! Where have you been?' she asked. She was looking tired and worn. Until the war she had always been smartly dressed, her fair hair carefully set by a hair dresser every week. Now it often fell about her face, and she had acquired a new gesture of throwing it away from her face with the backs of her wrists.

'I've been fetching Kensington,' Gillian answered, dancing past towards the back door leading into the garden. 'Come and see them introduced.'

'But, darling, I told you not to stay out more than half an hour. You know we don't want you away –' The voice faded behind Gillian, lost in the high-ceilinged hall. Rosemary had to meet her new companion.

The two rabbits, the white and the grey, might have known one another all their lives, only exchanging indifferent glances and cursory sniffs, and then hopping off about the cage in search of odd scraps of food. Animals could be disappointing sometimes. Gillian stood back watching them for a few moments, hoping that they were perhaps shy in front of a human of showing their delight at seeing one another.

Her mother came up quietly behind her. 'She is pretty,' she said. 'What did you say her name was?'

'Kensington. Can I let them out to play in the garden?'

'Not now. She really is a female, isn't she, darling? Kensington sounds very distinguished, but hardly a feminine name, surely? You know you did promise that this one would be a girl.' She was bending over the cage anxiously examining the white rabbit. 'We just can't cope with any more babies, Gillian, especially just now.'

'I've called her Kensington,' Gillian said again patiently. 'She could hardly be a boy with a pretty name like that.'

Her mother could reasonably have pointed out that Rosemary's last companion had been called Prunella, but that had not stopped Rosemary from having twenty-eight babies in twelve months, twenty-six of which had had to be let free on the Downs, saturated in eau de Cologne in case the wild rabbits should catch the smell of humans on their fur and kill them. The other two Gillian had exchanged in the market (with 3s. 6d.) for Kensington – a real girl this time, the market man had assured her.

Mrs Hartford undid the knot in her apron string and slipped the apron over her arm. 'Come along, it's lunch time. Grilled lamb chops,' she added with the touch of pride of someone who has not been cooking for long. The living-in maid, who did most of the cooking, too, had left and Gillian's mother was now a twelve-hour-a-day housewife.

They had lunch in the basement kitchen, and after helping their mother to wash up, Gillian, Drake, and Sammy retired upstairs for their half-hour reading time. They could read where they liked, and that meant that they usually sprawled about in Drake's front bedroom, which overlooked the gardens and sea, and talked

15

rather than read. It was the one time of the day during the holidays when the three children were together before dispersing to their different friends and different occupations.

Drake, at fourteen, considered himself too old for the family siesta and that it was his privilege to wander off before the half-hour was up or to continue reading (usually a heavy book on advanced biology) until tea time if he felt so inclined.

Gillian was beginning to despair of Drake, who was lying stretched out on his back on his bed under the window, a large blue-bound book at arms' length. As recently as last summer, Drake could be relied upon for the wildest expeditions, and for being as untidy and forgetful as she was. But Drake had unaccountably changed. He had acquired the habit of putting things away and remembering the times of meals. He also appeared to do as much work at home as he did at school.

All of which, Gillian grudgingly admitted, was probably admirable, but certainly did not make him a more exciting person. She supposed that it was (like the new soft down on his upper lip) something to do with growing up. Last summer he would have waded into the Foulshams, fists flailing in the proper manner. But the other day 'the sheer authority of my presence' as he

16

jokingly described it afterwards, had been enough to send them slinking off.

'I met the foolish Foulshams this morning,' Gillian said, and she had to repeat it before Drake would look up from his book. Their father was the same. Gillian supposed that all doctors had to be spoken to twice before they would take any notice of what was being said to them, though she thought Drake was picking up the habit rather early.

'Did they catch you?' he asked, suddenly anxious.

'They did and they didn't,' Gillian told him. 'A soldier armed with goodness knows what saved me – and off they went with their tails between their legs. I could have got away easily if I hadn't had Kensington with me. And do you know what?' she demanded, her brown eyes bigger than ever, and starting a little dance of indignation, 'they had the cheek to say that Kensington was theirs.'

Drake put his book aside, rolled off the bed and stood up, a square, stocky figure in flannel trousers and a blue, long-sleeved jersey. He rested his hands on the windowsill, his fingers splayed out on the chipped woodwork; long, thin fingers like his father's. He was staring thoughtfully at the Foulshams' house across the gardens on the other side of Lewes Crescent. It was a house very similar to theirs, a Regency terrace house of four floors, distinguished by the shade of deep yellow in which George Foulsham had had it painted.

'Well, we shan't have to worry about them much longer, that's something,' Drake said. 'Though I suppose when this invasion scare is over and we come back again, they'll still be there. Obviously nothing is going to shift that mad father of theirs from his studio.'

George Foulsham (Mrs Foulsham had died when Simon had been born) was considered to be famous for his surrealist landscapes and still lifes. In Brighton one heard a lot about these, and little about the very highly finished paintings he did to illustrate romantic stories in women's magazines, though it was the money he earned from these that paid for all eight children to go to a very wild 'do-as-you-like' boarding school. George Foulsham claimed to be a loving father, often speaking of the £1,500 a year he had to pay in school fees; and, as he explained to friends, the greatest kindness you can do to children is to take no notice of them. 'Give them their freedom, that's the gist of my educational philosophy,' he had often been heard to say. And this included the freedom to persecute Gillian and her younger brother, Sammy, chasing them about the sea front and the gardens, shouting after them down the streets of Kemp Town, and attacking them physically whenever they got the chance. To the Foulshams, the Hartford family were a lot of over-respectable prigs. 'Foul conformists!' Gillian often had shouted at her, though she had never understood what it meant. The feud had been going on for years.

Gillian stood by her brother at the window, easing up on to the tips of her toes and down again, impatient with her brother's silent contemplation and anxious to be off doing something. Even when she was not on tip-toe she was a full inch taller than Drake, taking after her mother, who was five feet ten inches. They could just make out the white-overalled figure of George Foulsham working at his easel in the first-floor bedroom that he used for a studio.

'Did they catch you?' Gillian spun round at the sound of Sammy's voice; Drake turned more slowly and retired back to his bed and his book. 'I saw them tearing off after you,' went on Sammy, who had two books under his arm because he had nearly finished *Jutland: the Failure of a Fleet*. 'I was watching the destroyers turning about on their patrol line and beating their way west again.'

'If you'd bothered to come and help,' Gillian answered with some scorn, 'you would have seen me beating my way down the cliffs with that pack of lunatics after me.' Until Drake had become all serious and bound up with his work, there had been at least one man of action in the family. Now it was all doctoring and naval theory.

'Sorry,' said Sammy, who was only too aware of his deficiencies as a tough fighting boy, although in fact, when his temper was aroused, Sammy sometimes surprised himself with what he could do with his fists.

Gillian was at the open window again, looking across the rolling lawns of the gardens to the yellow house. '*Their* rabbit indeed! As if any of them would keep a rabbit – except to eat it in a pie!' she spat out. 'I know,' she continued suddenly, spinning round and starting some complicated gyrations on the bedroom carpet, 'let's organize a raid on the Foulshams before we go. Get on to their roof at night, climb down into their loft when they're all in bed, and –'

Sammy was trying to take some interest, and even reluctantly raised his eyes from the pages of the book he had opened; but Drake was lying on his back again, deep in a chapter on hibernation. 'Oh, I give you two up,' she finished in disgust, pulled down a book at random from Drake's shelves, and threw herself at full length on to the rug.

2

The Thundery Joke

SOME time after it was all over, Sammy called it 'the thundery joke morning'; but that was later, when they could laugh at it. At the time nobody thought of it as a joke at all.

They were all doing different things when it started.

Gillian was standing on *one* hand on the lawn, Kensington and Rosemary hopping about contentedly near her. Neither of the rabbits appreciated her achievement. Gillian's bare feet were wandering about uncertainly, striving to balance her body in this unnatural position; her left arm was held slightly bent at the elbow a few inches above the ground, aching to give support to the other arm which so badly needed it.

'Now. . . !' Gillian succeeded in slightly bending her right arm, her nails digging deep into the grass, and struggled to get some spring into it. With an awful effort, she just managed to raise her hand from the ground, and with it her whole body, and then collapsed in a tumbled heap. How on earth had that clown managed it? He had walked half round the ring on one hand, in the most effortless way imaginable.

It was while she was lying on the lawn, staring up at the deep blue sky, clear but for a few vapour trails from high-flying aircraft, that she heard the thunder. It was very like any ordinary thunder except that it went on for a long time, rising and falling in intensity, sometimes fading away entirely and then becoming much louder and nearer. Gillian did not mind a good thunderstorm; her only worry was for her rabbits. Perhaps her mother would allow her to take them up to her bedroom until it was over.

The lawn had been mown the evening before by Drake; the grass smelt sweet and some of the clippings were sticking to her hot face. The planes had veered away to the east, trailing twelve white criss-crossing lines in the sky. Kensington was sitting up on her haunches, cocked ears twitching to the reverberant boom of the thunder; while Rosemary, who was never very adventurous, was nibbling beside the open cage door.

'Gillian!' Mrs Hartford was calling from Sammy's bedroom window.

Gillian hoisted herself on to her elbows and looked up. There was an odd note in her mother's voice as she called again. 'Come in darling. At once. Where are Drake and Sammy? Have you seen them?'

But before Gillian could answer her mother had disappeared. She stretched out a hand to Kensington and gently held her soft white back. The rabbit made no attempt to struggle as she was lifted and carried back to her cage.

'Don't worry, you can come out again soon,' Gillian reassured her as she reached down for Rosemary.

Sammy was sitting on his bicycle at the lock gates at Shoreham harbour, watching the destroyer slicing its way slowly through the still water towards him. It was an 'S' class vessel – 1,490 tons, four 4.7-inch guns, eight 21-inch torpedo tubes amidships, top speed 35 knots: Sammy would have known that if it had been five miles out to sea. It was not for nothing that Sammy Hartford memorized the specifications of every warship in the world from *Jane's Fighting Ships*. The displacement and secondary armament of a Venezuelan gun-boat? Sammy could rattle them off without a pause for thought. Once trains were the only thing that had mattered in his life, and he had been as great a locomotive authority then as he was a naval expert now. But that seemed a long time ago.

He heard the bell ring down to the engine-room for half-astern, watched the bow wave fall as the ship slowed, pointing its prow straight towards the open lock gate. There were half a dozen bluejackets at the bows, curled ropes ready for casting ashore held in the hands of two of them – tough, tanned, neat figures, completely sure of what they were doing. Sammy never tired of watching them go about their duties on board as their ships left harbour, and especially the way they brought them through the lock with such complete self-assurance. He always found it a tonic to come down to the harbour, where he spent most of his days during the holidays, to watch the ships coming in and going out; or to help the fishermen on the beach. But it was perhaps also a rather bitter tonic because his father had told him (gently and kindly) that, because of his eyesight, it was very unlikely that he could ever be a sailor. For Sammy wore spectacles, had worn them since he was four.

The destroyer was half into the lock, the sailors calling out to the lock-keeper and his men as they ran the heavy ropes round the bollards, before Sammy noticed with a start that the anti-aircraft guns on the bridge wings were manned by gun crews. They were wearing steel helmets, and were swinging the barrels of their multiple pom-

24

poms as they peered keenly up at the sky. The officers on the bridge were wearing steel helmets too.

Sammy had seen photographs of warships cleared for action with the crew at battle stations, but had never seen it in real life before. Of course they were at war, had been for months; but to be at battle stations while your ship was going through a harbour lock was very unusual; Sammy knew that.

When the destroyer was in the lock there was a slight delay in closing the gate behind it. 'Make it snappy, Mac – they're on the way,' the captain called out to the lock-keeper; and the gates swung to, enclosing the ship tightly in its crate of stone and concrete. At once the water began to pour out through the sluices at the sea end of the lock, and the long, grey, purposeful-looking vessel fell with the water, until its bridge was on a level with the top of the lock.

Sammy wheeled his bicycle up to the brink of the lock and looked along the deck in fascination, drinking in the sight of the 4.7-inch guns behind their splinter-shields, the radio aerial antennae, deck houses and Carley floats, the torpedo tubes, which were loaded, he noticed, with torpedoes – all the paraphernalia that make up the complicated organism of a fighting vessel. From below decks he could hear the gentle rumble of the destroyer's powerful turbines.

'Coming for a sunny cruise, sonny?'

Sammy smiled at the grinning sailor who had called out to him, and tried to wink back. He wished he could wink properly and could wisecrack as smartly at the sailors who called out to him when their ships passed through the lock. Some of the boys who hung about the lock cracked jokes as easily as the sailors and gave as good as they got.

This time Sammy was saved from having to find an answer, for at that moment the thunder began, booming and reverberating from along the coast, filling the air with its vibrations. At once everyone's attention was turned towards it, and the lock men at the bollards swung round and stared east beyond the big cranes and warehouses and oil-storage tanks of the harbour.

'Come on, Mac, get those gates open,' the captain called out through a megaphone. 'Now you see why we're in a hurry.'

The sailor who had winked at Sammy turned to him again before his ship slipped out of the lock and said more seriously, 'You'd better get home, sonny.'

'Why, what's the matter?' Sammy asked.

'Nasty storm coming up – don't you hear it?'

Sammy could hear it all right but was rather offended that anyone should think he might be scared of a thunderstorm.

'*Coming for a sunny cruise, sonny?*'

'Why are you in such a hurry, then?' he asked.

The destroyer's propellers were churning the water up into white froth at her stern and the sailor at his gunpost was already twenty feet away. He was grinning again, Sammy saw, and he gave a last wink that creased up the whole of his tanned face as he called out mysteriously, 'Any port in a storm, you know the saying.'

Sammy was still puzzling over these last words as he pedalled slowly along the cinder track that led on to the main Brighton coast road, while behind him the destroyer was already cutting her way into the rough water at the mouth of the river estuary.

The thunder was echoing back from the walls of the boat-builders' yards between which Sammy was bicycling. It seemed to be going on for a curiously long time and he hoped he would get home before the storm broke; not because he minded thunderstorms or worried about getting wet, but because he had been told not to go beyond the Palace Pier. 'I don't want you to be far away from home just now,' his mother had said. If he arrived back at Lewes Crescent soaking wet, it would be clear that he had bicycled farther than that.

Sammy had gone some way along the sea front and was almost into Hove before he realized that there was an unusual number of people about, and that they all appeared to be in a hurry.

Over the past weeks he had become accustomed to the silent empty streets, the shut-up houses and shops and the general air of emptiness and neglect in Brighton and Hove. Only a few buses had continued running, and there had been almost no cars about.

It was a surprise to discover how many people were still living in the two towns after all. Hove sea front was almost as thick with people as it was at the height of the August holiday season. But instead of ambling along the lawns and beaches with their dogs and children, all these people were rushing about in a state of alarm. Instead of calling out to one another and laughing and playing, as the holiday-makers did, these men and women were silent – silently hurrying along the streets. And instead of carrying beach towels and picnic baskets and spades and balls, they were bent under the weight of swollen suitcases or were pushing prams piled with luggage of all kinds.

'What a curious sort of morning this is!' Sammy thought to himself as he bicycled along close to the kerb, watching a worried-looking woman locking her front door and then helping her husband out through the gate with a cabin trunk. They dropped it clumsily on the path in their hurry and quickly snatched it up again, all without a word.

Sammy had never seen so many people in such a

hurry in all his life. Up the side streets leading away from the sea towards the centre of the town, the same scenes were taking place, and here the crowds were so thick that the people were spilling off the pavements on to the roads. Sammy could see men wheeling bicycles and hand trolleys loaded high with bits of furniture and bundles of sheets and blankets and curtains. It was as if the town had been poked with a stick, as you poke one of those innocent-looking soft pyramids of pine needles in a forest, and all the people had poured forth like ants from their nest.

A van came slowly towards Sammy; it was the only vehicle in sight on the sea front except a distant armoured car dashing in the opposite direction. On its roof was a loudspeaker, from which a voice called out above the sound of the continuing thunder. 'Make your way to the station, please, everyone,' the voice was saying. 'Don't rush, remain calm. There will be plenty of trains.' There was a short pause, and then the announcement began all over again with, 'We are putting into effect the emergency evacuation order. Make your way to the station, please, everyone. . . .'

The loudspeaker van was almost opposite Sammy when it swung across the road and slowed down beside him. A uniformed figure thrust his head through the open window. 'What do you think you're up to, boy? This is no time for joy-riding. You'd better get to the station right away. Dump your bicycle and follow everyone else. You can pick up your parents later.'

Sammy slowed down, listening in astonishment to these orders.

'But I'm going home for lunch,' he said. What an extraordinary idea! Why on earth should he dump his bicycle?

'We are putting into effect the emergency evacuation order,' repeated the official like a parrot, the words sounding quite different now that they were spoken in an ordinary voice instead of being amplified by the loudspeaker. 'You hop off and do as you're told.'

For a moment Sammy thought the official was going to get out, snatch the bicycle from him, and send him off with the crowds. Suddenly he realized the moment for drastic action had arrived. He jammed on his brakes so that the van slid ahead, and then pressing down on to the pedals with all his strength, shot past on the outside and raced ahead.

There might have been a distant cry of 'Hey you, stop!' Sammy was not sure. He flew along the wide smooth road as fast as he could go, towards the West Pier and the towering hotels that marked the beginning of Brighton, without looking behind him.

He was by now thoroughly scared. What did the official mean, 'You can pick up your parents later?' His mother and father, and Drake and Gillian, would be getting ready for lunch at Adelaide House . . . in the afternoon he had thought of bicycling along to Newhaven. There was always an interesting assortment of ships at Newhaven.

The wide streets of the Old Steine were black with people, an urgent, hurrying, scurrying crowd, two or three loaded buses blowing their horns as they tried to squeeze through them. Sammy left them behind and pedalled up the short hill on to the Marine Parade.

It was less than a mile to home now. Out at sea, beyond the Palace Pier, he could still make out the low shape of the destroyer, tearing eastwards, trailing a thin line of grey smoke, and he wondered what the winking sailor was doing now.

The noise of the thunder was becoming even louder, and yet there were no dark clouds building up from the direction of the storm – only a faint smoke haze that hung over the sea off Newhaven harbour seven miles away, like a patch of mist. Every few moments the mist appeared to light up with brief white flashes like sudden darts of flame in a smoky fire, which Sammy at first thought must be lightning.

But even if he was not yet ten, Sammy realized just before he turned off into Lewes Crescent that this was no ordinary thunderstorm: the lightning was too frequent, the thunder too continuous, for that. Thunderstorms did not hover about like a local sea mist in one spot; they filled the sky with black clouds and brought rain with them.

He stopped his bicycle for one last look at the destroyer before turning up his road. When he saw the sparkles from the two forward guns, and heard the sudden cracks like ripping paper a few seconds later, he understood why the captain had been in such a hurry; and that the dull booming that had filled his ears for the last half-hour was certainly not the sound of thunder.

Drake had the best view on 'the thundery joke morning'. He had worked in his bedroom until eleven o'clock, and then told his mother that he was going out to stretch his legs.

'Don't go too far, darling,' Mrs Hartford said. 'I don't really like any of you leaving the house with things as they are. Goodness knows what Sammy's up to.'

Drake walked down the front steps one at a time. 'Oh come, Mother, don't bracket me with Sammy. I'm a little more responsible than he is, you know,' he called back from the pavement. 'Anyway, we'll hear in plenty of time if anything does happen.' He spoke tolerantly, patiently, in his newly-broken voice. One had to make allowances, he told himself. It was, after all, an anxious time for Mother, and she was working much too hard.

At the end of the Parade he cut up across the grass to the cliff-tops above Black Rock. It was the nearest open country to Lewes Crescent, brisk and invigorating, with short, springy turf underfoot, but spoilt now by the new zigzag trenches cut into the grass and the barbed-wire entanglements which sprang up like ugly steel hedges every few hundred yards. It was forbidden territory to civilians, but Drake had got to know many of the soldiers stationed up on the cliffs, and now he could wander along whenever he felt inclined, stopping to chat with the men in the dugout gunposts. Sometimes he played chess with a corporal called Harry.

On that morning most of the soldiers had their shirts off and were sprawling about in the heat in their vests, their tin hats tipped forward over their eyes while they played cards, read the newspapers, or just smoked. A group of them were bent over the engine of an armoured car which was refusing to start.

Drake sat down as Harry walked over to join them with the pocket chess set under his arm. 'Any news?' he asked the corporal.

'Immediate readiness, double watches to be kept, enemy attack expected in twenty-four hours,' Harry said wearily. 'Same as yesterday and the day before and the day before that. Jerry'll never come, take it from me. Your turn to be black,' he added, as he set out the men on the little board. He was just putting the white king in place when the first clap of thunder burst out.

All the soldiers swung round together in the direction of the sound – all except the lugubrious Harry. 'Only a spot of thunder – what's the panic about a storm?' he asked.

The sound of the thunder increased, rolling over the Downs beyond. Drake stood up on the gun emplacement and stared east up Channel.

'Funny sort of storm, Harry,' a private murmured. 'Seems to be raining invasion barges over Newhaven way. Take a look.'

There was a heat haze that reduced visibility over the sea to no more than ten miles, but they could all make out the little long shapes stealing in from the French shore beyond the horizon. There were dozens of them, too many to count, and mingled among them were the larger silhouettes of warships. As broadside after broadside was hurled over the advancing flotillas of barges and crashed out of sight on the shore, the warships' hulls were lit up by twinkling lines of muzzle flashes from their guns; and many seconds later the repeated booms reached their ears.

'Yep, this is it,' Harry commented with grim satisfaction. He had a hand on Drake's shoulder to keep his balance on the narrow concrete wall. All along the rolling cliff-tops the soldiers were standing in small bunches, staring silently out to sea. 'You'd better push off home, old lad,' he went on. 'Things are liable to get hot around here, and your Mum and Dad'll want you.' He glanced down at the chessboard lying on the grass. 'I'll tan you at that when we push Jerry back into the sea.'

Drake stood for a moment longer watching the start of the long-expected invasion, solemnly conscious of the historic importance of the moment. The first time since 1066! It was clear that they were going in at Newhaven at the wide estuary of the Ouse, and from the swarm of little dots in the sky above the town, the Stukas were preparing the way with a heavy dive-bombing attack. A cloud of smoke was rising from the scene of the battle, the density suggesting that a screen was being laid ahead of the invasion barges.

Harry was right; he ought to go home now. 'Good-bye,' he called as he jumped off the gun emplacement.

'Good luck, kid.'

Drake paused to put the chess-men back in their box – just as a gesture. 'I hope you get on all right,' were his last words to the group of watching men, and at once he realized how ridiculous they must have sounded to soldiers about to go into battle.

As Drake ran down the grassy slope at a brisk trot, he noticed that his legs were not working as well as usual. Every few steps his knees seemed to give and he would nearly stumble. He could not understand it at first; then he realized that it was caused by the excitement that was racing through him, and the violent feeling of being caught up in real war, of being a personal target for the enemy. 'Me, me – they're after ME, they want to kill ME!' kept passing through his mind as he made for home. It was an odd feeling, altogether different from the anger of petty feuds with the Foulshams or a scrap at school. There was something intimate and personal about it that brought out strange new emotions in him.

As a keen biologist, he was later able to recognize how he, as a human, must have lost the natural physical instincts of an animal. A hunted animal, he realized, doesn't stumble awkwardly when it runs; it runs swiftly and surely, every muscle tuned and tensed for the crisis. And a hunted animal thinks only of escape or the protection of its young; while Drake found his thoughts divided as he pounded on to the tarmac pavement and crossed the Marine Parade to Lewes Crescent. Half of him wanted to stay with the soldiers until they went into battle (perhaps to help tend the wounded – yes, that was what he would like to do) while the other half of his mind told him that he must help his mother and Sammy and Gillian. His father might be called on for emergency service in the Medical Corps, and certainly in the civilian ambulance brigade if Brighton were attacked. Then Drake would be in charge of the family.

Drake's legs appeared to be working normally again and he ran freely without stumbling on the last lap of his journey home across the gardens. He could see his mother and Gillian on the doorstep of Adelaide House. His father was walking rapidly towards the sea front as if in search of Sammy.

'Thank goodness, there you are darling!' his mother cried out when she caught sight of him. 'We can't find Sammy anywhere'; and she pushed back some loose strands of hair that had fallen over her face. Even Gillian, still in bare feet, showed some signs of anxiety.

'You know they've come, don't you?' Drake panted out when he reached the bottom of the steps. 'It looks as if they're landing at Newhaven.'

'You should hear the wireless,' Gillian said, her eyes wide with excitement. 'Talk about solemn. "There is no cause for alarm,"' she mimicked the cultured B.B.C. announcer. '"Our troops will resist strongly every attempt by the enemy to land on our coast." Well, so I should jolly well hope.'

'Don't be so stupid, Gillian,' Mrs Hartford snapped. 'This is no time for joking.' Drake noticed the knuckles of her restless fingers were white; so people really did wring their hands in distress. Then his mother suddenly tensed and started forward down the steps at a run. 'There he is – oh thank God!'

It was Sammy all right, making zigzag patterns in the gutter with the front wheel of his bicycle, while he walked up the road in deep conversation with his father. They might have been returning from a picnic on the beach.

There was no sign of strain or fear on their father's face; Drake noticed that at once and was very impressed.

After Sammy had suffered a kiss from his mother, Dr Hartford presided at an unofficial kerbside family conference, standing on the first step leading up to the house to give himself more height. He was, in fact, an inch shorter than his wife, and only a shade taller than Gillian: a reserved, austere, kindly man, whose contact with his children was through gentle and unemotional affection rather than close association. He was too busy to give them very much of his time.

'I'm afraid, we've got to leave a day early,' he told them in his soft voice. 'You can hear why.' And he smiled wanly and glanced in the direction of the gunfire. 'The whole of Brighton and Hove is being cleared by tonight – if the Germans give us time. They're trying to get everyone to go to the station now, but that will only mean a lot of waiting about in a crowd. So I think we'll have lunch first and go along this afternoon.'

'I can still take the rabbits, can't I?' Gillian asked anxiously.

'You can try. But you may not be allowed on the train with them.'

'There's no need to tell you not to be scared,' Dr Hartford ended, 'because obviously you aren't. I don't think there's any real danger. The Germans aren't anxious to kill civilians – and I'm sure they'll be sent back to where they came from, even if they do manage to get ashore.'

They filed up the steps and in through the front door. Before closing it behind him, Gillian glanced across at the Foulshams' house. It looked empty and lifeless, with all the windows closed. So they had left first after all.

A dozen Spitfire fighters flew east low overhead, the roar of their engines momentarily drowning the sound of the bombing and gunfire. . . .

3

The Kidnapping

'WE MUST be very careful to wash up beautifully,' Mrs Hartford said, with her hands deep in the kitchen sink, her head clouded with steam. 'Everything put away just so, no crumbs left about for mice. We must think of when we come back to the house again and how awful it would be to find things untidy. Like coming down in the morning after a late party. . . .'

She was talking incessantly, in a rather high, strained sort of voice, as she mopped the dishes in rapid succession and put them on to the draining board to be dried. Drake noticed that her apron was on askew; he saw the unnaturally high colour in her cheeks; recognized that she was talking without thought to avoid the risk of silence between them.

Drake's heart ached with sympathy for his mother. For Sammy and Gillian this sudden flight before the

Germans was nothing more than a rather frightening adventure. For his mother, who had read of the fearful experiences of Polish and French refugees in the war, this, Drake understood, was the realization of all her nightmares.

'I shouldn't worry about the mice,' Drake broke in with a laugh. 'We'll be back again before they turn up.' He hung the last cup on its dresser hook and glanced through the window at Gillian who was busy with Kensington and Rosemary at the end of the garden. 'I'll go and see how she's getting on with those boxes. I wish she would just let them loose in the garden; they're going to be an awful weight to carry.'

It was nearly four o'clock before they assembled in the hall with their luggage, the three children in their best clothes, their mother in a black coat and skirt.

'It's like going away for the summer holidays,' Gillian said lightly as she jumped the last three stairs and bent down to peer through the holes in Kensington's cardboard travelling box. 'I do hope she'll be all right. Such a shock for her just as she was getting used to the garden.'

'Is everything locked up, Drake?' Mrs Hartford asked. 'Water and electricity turned off? We're to meet Daddy at the station. He's helping to get the patients at the hospital off into ambulances.' She picked up two of the biggest suitcases, which Drake made her exchange for smaller ones, and led the way to the door. 'Come along now,' she told them, trying to make her voice sound brisk.

Gillian was the last to leave. Before slamming the front door she called out loudly and cheerfully, 'Goodbye, dear Adelaide House. We shan't be long.' Her voice echoed back from the silent rooms in the hollow, ghostly way of all sounds in deserted houses. None of them turned to look back at their house from the road.

It was a long, weary journey to the station, down Eastern Road, St George's Road and St James's Street towards the Old Steine. They halted frequently to rest their aching arms, to move suitcases from hand to hand, sometimes to exchange them between one another.

Always Drake tried to persuade his mother to carry only the small case Sammy was carrying, vainly attempting to stack two under each of his own arms. He kept saying fretfully, 'No, it's all right, I can manage,' while the perspiration stood out like raindrops on his forehead.

There were few people about now. Nearly everyone had answered the loudspeaker summonses from the touring vans and made their way at once to the station. But there were still one or two old men and women, helped by soldiers, piling their belongings on to carts and prams in the side streets. They looked intent and desperate.

No one could mistake the sounds of battle from the east for thunder any longer. The steady, continuous rumble was broken by frequent heavier explosions that shook the ground and set the doors of the empty shops rattling. When they halted on the pavement to rest, they could see the trails of many aircraft high above them, intertwined like the web of some demented spider; and they could hear the far-away rattle of the fighters' cannon and machine-gun fire. They were too tired to talk.

Parked ruthlessly in the middle of the lovely gardens in the Old Steine was a tank, its overalled crew standing round it. A dozen or more people, bunched into family groups and all carrying bags, were scurrying up towards North Street or the Pavilion heading for the station, and a last red doubledecker bus drove fast across the intersections, disregarding the red traffic lights.

In the centre of the gardens, the big, elaborate fountain was still playing away for the holiday-makers who had never come that year. But even as the Hartfords passed near it, its multitude of jets sank slowly, fizzled as if in a last effort to keep alive, and died to nothing.

The crowds became thicker as they approached the station, and there were uniformed civil defence officers lined along the street calling out in a cheerful way, 'It's all right, there'll be room for everyone.' 'Seats for all – and it's a free ride for all you lucky people today,' another officer shouted as they passed.

At the station approaches, where the people swarmed like bees at a hive entrance, the crowds were excited and talkative, as if after the anxious weeks of waiting for the worst, it was a relief to be facing the crisis at last. As they sat on their suitcases or moved a few steps nearer to the platforms inside, they swapped jokes, or pointed up at the aerial dog-fights taking place high above them, or asked one another for news. Everyone wanted to know what was happening, and anyone who talked loudly enough or spoke with authority was at once surrounded by a group of eager listeners.

'Chap in our street was on the last train out of Lewes,' a big man in a sweater standing near Gillian was saying. 'He said the Huns were half-way from Newhaven already. Our chaps running for their lives. . . .'

'Well, Jack here says he saw them from the cliffs being flung back into the sea – "Flung back" you said, didn't you, Jack.'

'The B.B.C. man said on the radio we're bringing up reinforcements and we're to keep calm. Calm, laugh I say! Who's panicking, that's what I'd like to know.'

A red-faced fisherman standing on his bulging suitcase like a soap-box orator had a good audience. 'It's a pince movement, that's what it is,' he shouted. 'The Germans are ashore at Worthing, too. Brighton's going to be pincered, you see. The old town's going to be like a nut in a nut cracker.'

'Oh, nuts!' roared out one of his listeners and burst into bellows of laughter.

All around the Hartfords the voices droned on, rising above one another, falling and rising again.

'Well, I think it's terrible, just terrible!' Sammy turned at the sound of the frail little voice and smiled at the old woman in a black dress sitting on the kerb with her budgerigar cage on her knees. His mother sat down beside her and began talking quietly as she held her hand.

The sun was falling low over the houses and shops to the west of the station before they arrived inside. Between snatches of dance music on the loudspeakers, announcements poured out over their heads. 'Don't worry, we'll have you all away before it's dark,' the voice kept telling the waiting crowds in an over-cheerful voice, 'and everything is arranged for you in London. There are emergency beds for the night, and for those who have no friends in the country, there are hostels ready for you. Two trains have just arrived in platforms five

46

and six. Please make your way to them as quickly as possible.'

Under the high station roof, the sounds of people calling to one another, of the steel-wheeled trolleys running along the platforms, of the hissing of steam from the old locomotives pressed into emergency service, echoed bewilderingly about them.

Gillian moved forward with the crowd, Kensington under her right arm, Rosemary tucked under her left arm. When they halted again she stooped and undid the string securing their cardboard boxes. 'You poor things – all this noise, and no air to breathe.'

Her mother stood above her, turning round on tiptoe, anxiously looking for her father. 'Don't worry, he's bound to be along in a minute,' Drake said. Lying in the farthest platform was a train of coaches, white-painted with the Red Cross on their side, and the sick from the town's hospitals were being carried in from ambulances. There were a lot of nurses and several doctors hovering about. Drake pointed towards them. 'Father will be over there, I'm sure,' he said, 'I'll run and tell him we're here.'

But Drake did not get far. Railway officials helped by civilian defence workers were shepherding the last few hundred people towards the waiting trains on the platforms, and Gillian saw one of them stop Drake and direct him back to his family. 'Sorry, madam,' he said firmly to Mrs Hartford, 'we can't have people straying about. This is an emergency, you know, and every second counts.' He glanced towards the nearest platform into which a train was arriving, the engine letting off steam with a great hissing. 'This is the last adult train, so make it snappy, madam,' he added, and swung away to steer the forlorn groups of waiting evacuees towards the barrier.

'Hurry along, please, hurry, hurry,' the loudspeakers boomed. 'This is the last –'

Crouching beside her rabbits, Gillian saw her mother suddenly start forward and run after the official. 'What do you mean, "adult train"?' she called frantically; and when the official disappeared she turned to a porter busily helping another group with their luggage. 'What does he mean, "adult" train? We're all together – I've got my three children with me.'

But her words were drowned by the voice from the loudspeaker and the sudden ear-splitting whistle from the engine, and the porter could only smile helplessly and shake his head to indicate that he could not hear.

Their mother rejoined them. 'I don't understand,' she said, her voice raised high. 'We're all travelling together, children. Come along.' Her frightened blue eyes flashed from Gillian to Sammy, and then to Drake as if seeking support. 'Come along,' she repeated, and her hands darted out to snatch the suitcases.

'Hurry along, please, hurry. This is the last adult train,' the announcer called out over and over again, louder and louder as if striving to make himself heard above the sudden crescendo of sound from the locomotives. Two were pulling out of the platforms, the last train was still letting off steam and sounding its whistle repeatedly.

The ordered calm that had prevailed until then was now broken, and the remaining passengers began running for the platform entrance, tripping over their luggage, pushing one another, knocking their cases against each other's legs, and forcing their way through the narrow entrance.

'It's all right – there's plenty of room,' the fat station-master at the barrier was shouting hoarsely, his face the colour of a blood-orange, while just above his head a loudspeaker continued calling out, 'Hurry, hurry please....'

Gillian struggled to keep behind Sammy, who was holding on to the tail of his mother's coat with one hand and his suitcase with the other. Men and women were bumping into them on all sides. 'Take it easy there,' 'Steady on now,' they were calling as they were pressed from the crush behind. The noise and the people seemed to be bearing down on to Gillian with a terrible weight, so that she thought she would be thrown to the ground at any moment and crushed to a pulp with her rabbits.

At the open platform gates six burly military policemen were helping the older people as they emerged staggering from the bottleneck. The corporal in charge reached out an arm and detached Sammy from his mother as he went past, and another policeman at his side called to Gillian and Drake, 'Here, you two. Not this one.'

At the sound of the voice, Mrs Hartford dropped her cases and swung round against the stream of hurrying people. Even Gillian would never forget the look on her face, the expression of frantic anxiety and sudden anger; and she would never forget the tone of her voice calling out in a high-pitched shriek above all the other sounds, 'But they're my children!'

'Sorry, ma'am,' the corporal answered her over the heads of the passengers tearing by, raising his voice louder and louder as Mrs Hartford was forced farther and farther away. 'Adults only on this train. No children on this one. But it'll be all right.' He was shouting now, 'DON'T WORRY, MA'AM. IT'S FOR THEIR OWN SAFETY.'

For a few seconds Gillian caught glimpses of her mother's fair head above the crush of people; then she was lost in the crowd which was shepherded firmly on to the train. And Drake and Sammy and she were left in the firm arms of the policemen, a little group washed up on the banks of a river in full flood.

The corporal was very kind. 'You'll see your Mum again soon,' he told them as the last carriage disappeared out of the platform. 'We had a special train for the kiddies early on. Safest earliest, the Colonel said. Any kiddies who turned up late is to travel on the Red Cross train. Those are our orders. A Red Cross train's always safe. No one would attack anything with a Red Cross on it.'

The station was empty of all but a scattering of officials. The corporal, with an arm on Sammy's and Gillian's shoulders, led them back through the barrier, while two more military policemen carried their luggage and the rabbits past the shuttered bookstalls and kiosks. 'You'd best stay in the waiting-room until the Red Cross train's ready. You'll find some more kids in, there – ones who got lost earlier on,' he said at the swing glass doors. 'Keep your peckers up.'

He gave them a grin in turn and walked briskly off with the other two, three stiff, upright figures whose boots went click-clack in time across the now silent station hall.

The fat stationmaster came hurrying up to Drake, puffing and blowing. 'They didn't ought to have done that, lad. Not split you up from your Mum like that, break her heart it will.' He paused for breath; he was a very worried man, Drake saw. 'We're letting a few stray kiddies go on the Red Cross train – but that was cruel, plain cruel. Take their orders too literal, these military gentlemen.'

'Never mind,' Drake said. 'I expect it'll be all right. We'll find her again in London. Anyway, it's done now.'

The stationmaster hobbled away, still looking flustered, still muttering, 'These military gentlemen ...' and Drake led the way into the waiting-room, pushing open the doors with the suitcases he had reclaimed from the soldiers. 'Poor Mother,' he was thinking, 'she'll be worrying herself sick.' He could imagine her feelings on the journey to London, with many halts, in the blacked-out train. If only Father had turned up in time. But he would probably be travelling on the Red Cross train with them now.

It was almost dark in the musty old waiting-room. The black-out curtains were already pulled down and it was lit by only one naked bulb; but there were little groups of children, all frightened and some crying, huddled about the wooden benches along the walls.

'Well, look who's here, if it isn't those dear old Hartfords.' At the sound of the mocking voice, Drake glanced towards the bunch of children lounging about the empty fireplace on the far side of the waiting-room. So the Foulshams had missed the children's train, too. There they were, all eight of them, as noisily unrepressed as ever.

Drake turned to Gillian and Sammy and told them to put down their cases by the door. 'Just don't take any notice of them,' he said quietly. 'They'll soon dry up.' This was no time or place to start a shouting match with those tiresome, juvenile Foulshams.

But they were not to be left in peace. With the big, red-headed Arthur in the lead as usual, and glancing from side to side to make sure all the other waiting children were watching, they strode over to the new arrivals. 'So we're going to have the pleasure of the company of the horrid Hartfords on our desperate journey on the iron-road.' There was a broad smile on Arthur's freckled, chubby cheeks. 'Well I must say, that's going to raise the tone. Doubtless you're travelling first class, too?'

'Oh, dry up,' Drake answered, turning his back. 'Why don't you grow up?'

Arthur swept his arm over the heads of the Hartfords and swung round like a circus lion-tamer concluding his act. 'And all in their Sunday best,' he told his brothers and sisters. 'What a privilege!'

Eleanor, who had been looking over their luggage carefully, suddenly sprang forward, her hair spreading

wildly. 'And they've got their bunny-wuns with them –
do look, Arthur.'

Before Gillian could stop her she had stooped down
and undone the bow securing Kensington's cardboard
box. Quickly she raised the lid and peered inside, and at
once slid away the box across the floor, covering it with
her arms. 'It's Van Gogh!' she shouted triumphantly. 'I
thought so. Quick, all of you. I've got him.'

Within seconds a minor riot had developed in the
waiting-room. Gillian leapt forward with a cry of
anger, was pushed back by Arthur, Drake sprang up to
defend her, calling out, 'Give that back, you idiot!' while
the rest of the Foulshams surged round the captured
rabbit, screaming like a pack of hounds at the kill. In the
centre of them, Eleanor held the crate above her head
chanting, 'Dear old Van Gogh, back with his rightful
owners.'

'Silence! Silence, do you hear?' Drake shouted over
and over again, climbing on to a case to give himself
more height and authority. His eyes were blazing, his
dark cheeks had turned to a deep red colour; but no one
took any notice of him.

Sammy was the first to go into the mêlée, shooting
forward silently and head first, with all the force he
could muster, disregarding Drake's cry of 'Come back.'
Sammy was oblivious to everything. He knew only that a

terrible injustice had been committed and that Gillian's rabbit must be rescued.

For a moment Drake hesitated, watching his younger brother tearing his way through the kicking legs towards the centre of the scrum, his spectacles already torn off. Then, just as Gillian was scrambling to her feet to rejoin the fray, he took a flying leap. . . .

It was a tremendous and exhilarating and wonderful fight while it lasted. To Drake, Gillian, and Sammy, struggling against hopeless odds, it seemed that they were punching and gripping, throwing and being thrown for at least five minutes. But the best of it was over in less than a minute, during which time Gillian twice got her hands on Kensington's box, only to have it snatched away from her by superior forces.

Arthur and all the other Foulshams, especially Simon, shouted at their work; while the Hartfords fought silently and intently. Around them the anxious spectators increased the volume of their wailing.

From her position on the floor, on to which she had been thrown again by Jeremy Foulsham, and the youngest girl, Rosetti, Gillian caught a glimpse of the swing doors opening, and recognized the bare, plump legs that sped through them as belonging to Eleanor. She could only be flying for one reason: she must have the rabbit box.

'Quick – there she goes'

With a tremendous effort, Gillian managed to throw off the two children on top of her, thrust her way through the others jostling and swaying around her, and made off in pursuit. 'She's got her! Quick – there she goes,' she panted out to Drake and Sammy.

She threw aside the doors swinging towards her and broke out into the station hall, where two military policemen standing under the clock glanced in surprise in her direction. There was no one else in sight in the dark, empty station – only the distant figure of Eleanor Foulsham, her hair flying out behind her, disappearing round a pillar and on towards the twilit streets.

Gillian felt sure she could catch her. She was a very fast runner, the fastest in her school under fifteen; and a determined anger drove her on, while Eleanor was much heavier and was further handicapped by the weight of the rabbit.

Across the station forecourt she gained half a dozen yards and was almost close enough to clutch at her baggy sweater, when Eleanor suddenly doubled back unexpectedly into the Trafalgar Street tunnel that ran under the station approach.

In here it was almost pitch dark, and Gillian could only tell from the patter of sandals on tarmac ahead of her that Eleanor had crossed the road. The others, if they were following, were far behind; there was no other sound above that of her own heavy breathing and of the double footsteps racing down the steep hill.

When they emerged into the half-light again, she saw that Eleanor had re-crossed the road. They both turned sharply, only a few yards separating them again, into a narrow cobbled side street. She almost had her now. One last effort, one more burst of speed, and she could grab at the arm clutching the box – though she would have to be careful not to cause it to fall. . . .

She saw Eleanor turn her head and look back, her square little face a flaming red from the exertion of the pursuit, her open mouth gulping air.

A second later she caught sight of the bicycle leaning against the railings just ahead of them, and guessed what was going to happen before Eleanor's left arm reached out for it and knocked it crashing backwards across the pavement behind her.

But Gillian was too late to prevent herself from running headlong into it. Her feet caught in the frame and sent her sprawling helplessly forwards on to the pavement to the screaming sound of scraping metal.

It is surprising what you can suffer and survive without a thought in a crisis. At any other time Gillian, accustomed to falls as she was, would have given herself a moment to consider her injuries. But now she merely untangled the bicycle from her legs, kicked it aside and sprang to her feet again.

The street was empty. In that brief, stunning moment Eleanor and the rabbit had quite disappeared. Gillian hesitated, looked back to see if her brothers or more of the Foulshams were in sight, and ran forward again, glancing from side to side. It was a mean, sad little street of terrace houses, and the narrow alleyway cut into one side was invisible until you were almost on it. This was Eleanor Foulsham's only possible escape route, Gillian decided, as she felt her way into the dark entrance, limping slightly from a bruised knee, and aware for the first time of the pain shooting up her leg. And there seemed to be a good chance that it led to a dead end – and that she had her trapped.

It was a small timber-merchant's yard. Gillian could just make out in the last light of the summer evening the stacked planks and poles rising high above her on either side, and could smell the fresh scent of sawdust in the air. There was a row of little glass-fronted offices on one side, and there were several hand-carts and a truck parked in the centre of the yard: a difficult place to search without a light.

Oh, if only Drake were here! She hadn't the breath to shout, even lacked the strength to climb the ladders to peer along the lengths of timber.

Gillian was still standing under the yard's signboard at the entrance, panting and wondering what she should do next, when she heard Drake's distant voice calling her name. She ran back into the street. 'Here I am – quick. I've got her trapped,' her cry echoing back from the dark rows of houses.

His voice was nearer next time he called, and a few seconds later she saw his stocky figure running along the pavement towards her. He jumped over the fallen bicycle and followed Gillian into the timber-yard.

'She's hiding in here somewhere,' Gillian told her brother. 'She can't have got away. I'll stand at the entrance and you dig her out. Where are the others?' she asked.

From half-way up a ladder, peering along the lengths of timber, Drake called down, 'They scattered all over the place. Some of them were behind me, trying to hold back Sammy. I hope to goodness he's all right.' He was at the top of the ladder now. 'We'd no idea which way you went. Just luck I came down the hill. I can't see a thing up here – too dark.' He began climbing down again, rung by rung, and then made his way over to the offices. 'Locked,' he said, trying the doors in turn. 'Can't be in here. Let's take a look at the back of the place.'

With Drake leading, they felt their way along a narrow passage between planks and poles and sheets of hardboard and three-ply, tripping and stumbling in the darkness. Suddenly, as if emerging from a cave, they found themselves standing in another street.

'Huh, tradesmen's entrance!' Drake laughed. 'Fooled again.'

He took it more calmly than Gillian, who upbraided herself bitterly. 'What a fool!' she said over and over again. 'How could I be such an idiot? Poor, poor Kensington.'

'Never mind,' Drake said with a touch of impatience, aware for the first time that he had become involved in a somewhat undignified and fruitless wild goose chase. 'We're going to be travelling on the same train together. We'll get it back from her, don't worry.'

'Oh, don't always call my rabbits "it",' Gillian said crossly, near to tears.

It took them some time to find Sammy. They must have walked up and down a dozen streets, and Drake even ran down to the bottom of Trafalgar Street to St Peter's Church, calling his name every few minutes, before they decided to return to the station. 'He may have gone back there to wait for us,' he said, trying to put some conviction into his voice. 'Did you see him boring into them when the fight started? Our Sammy's not so mild as he looks when he's worked up about something.'

Gillian did not answer. They were emerging from the road tunnel into the station forecourt again. There was no sound above the distant rumble of battle from the east; no light except a flickering ruddy glow, reflecting from the clouds above Race Hill.

'Sammy, where are you?' Drake called out for the hundredth time.

Suddenly the dim glow blazed up more fiercely, like a prolonged flash of lightning, revealing with sudden clarity the front of the deserted station, the roadway and wide pavement leading to the booking-offices and hall, which had so recently been packed with crowds of refugees.

'Hullo, here I am.' At the same moment that they heard Sammy's calm, cheerful voice, they saw him sitting hunched up on the kerb beneath the long row of pillars. He got up and walked across the forecourt to meet them, looking oddly vulnerable without his spectacles, Drake noticed; it was remarkable what a difference they made.

'Did you catch her?' Sammy greeted them, and when Gillian shook her head, added, 'What a nuisance. I'm afraid Kensington's lost then.'

'What do you mean?' Gillian asked. 'We'll get her back on the train. They can't really *steal* her.'

The dimmed lights in the station hall were out now and there was nothing to guide them through the alley past the booking-offices. In the huge, high-roofed building there was not a glimmer of light, not the whisper of a sound. The station was like a factory that has been closed down for weeks.

'I think the last train must have gone,' Sammy said, still calm and apparently unaffected by the eerie silence of the hall. 'I came in a few minutes ago before you got back and it was like this.'

4

A Diet of Candy Floss

THE saddest sight he had ever seen met Sammy's eyes when he first opened them in the early morning of the day after the invasion. From the hard waiting-room bench on which he had slept, he could see out through one of the soot-stained windows into the great hall of Brighton station.

Never in its life of just a hundred years had it looked like this before: empty of engines, carriages, and freight wagons; empty of porters and passengers, cabs and trucks. It was quite dead. And a dead station is the deadest thing in the world.

The only moving things that Sammy could see as he hitched himself up on to one elbow (and he could not see them very well because he was still without his spectacles) were some fragments of litter blowing about in the morning breeze and the swinging shutter of a kiosk called Henry for Your Sweets and Cigarettes, which had broken loose.

Sammy, who was always the laziest Hartford in the mornings, lay down again on the seat with his head on the rolled-up coat, and decided to go to sleep again. But he was cold and his stomach ached with emptiness and his bones ached from lying on the hard wood. There was also a good deal to think about, which made it even more difficult to doze.

So he opened his eyes again, and while he watched Rosemary speculatively hopping about the waiting-room floor, thought about the fight and pursuit of the evening before, sadly about his mother's obvious distress at losing them, excitedly about that memorable sight of the destroyer racing into battle. Perhaps if they went down to the sea front they might see a full-scale naval engagement.

Thinking over the day that lay ahead with a good deal of satisfaction, Sammy swung his legs off the bench, leant down to give Rosemary a passing pat, and went out through the swing doors into the station hall.

Henry's kiosk was extraordinarily small inside. 'Fancy having to work all day in here,' he said aloud.

There was not much light and he could not read very well without his spectacles, but he succeeded in finding six small milk chocolate bars which he put in his pocket, placed a shilling (they were twopence each) in the open empty till, and wandered back across the silent hall.

'HAH!' he called as loudly as he dared before re-entering the waiting-room; and the echo came back satisfactorily from the high arched roof.

Drake and Gillian, awake now, followed him across the floor with their eyes.

'I've brought some breakfast. Would you like some?' Sammy asked politely.

Drake was rather severe and firm after they had eaten the chocolate. 'We'll take our luggage down to the Royal Albion Hotel and report to the army headquarters there,' he said. 'They'll look after us until they can put us in a truck or a staff car to London. I shouldn't think the Germans have cut us off from London yet. I'll ask them to telephone so that Father and Mother will know we're safe. Gillian, listen to me,' he said sharply, 'and leave that animal alone for a minute. You don't seem to realize this is serious.'

He was cross because he knew that this was all his fault really; they should never have dashed off like that and missed the train.

Gillian sat down on her suitcase with Rosemary on her lap. '*You* don't seem to realize she's starving,' she said. 'How would you like to go without any supper or breakfast?'

'I have. Now put it in its box and come on. We'll find some grass for it on the way. All right, sorry,' he corrected himself with a reluctant smile, 'we'll find *her* some grass.'

One cheerful discovery was that of Sammy's spectacles, lying miraculously unharmed under the waiting-room table. Gillian discovered them. 'It was really Rosemary, you must thank her,' she said as she handed them to him. Sammy wiped the lenses on the seat of his trousers, slipped them on thankfully – and the world took on a more familiarly clear-cut appearance.

They walked down Queen's Road in the rain. It did not seem quite right to walk in the middle of the road; they tried it once or twice, but always came back to the pavement. Outside a newsagent's, Sammy stopped and put down his case, his eye caught by the familiar coloured front page of his favourite comic on a rack that still hung by the door. Drake said, 'I suppose so,' when Sammy asked him if he thought it was all right to take it. The headlines on the damp newspapers above read, 'Invasion Threat Diminishes'. He put twopence through the letterbox and followed the others, walking slowly as he tried to read the front-page strip of 'Nelson, Hero of Trafalgar'.

Down North Street, which had many interesting shops, there were more diversions, and Drake had to keep calling them on. Outside a cinema the stills of a particularly exciting-looking Western were displayed, and, venturing curiously past the box office, Sammy discovered that the manager had forgotten to lock up in his hurry to leave. 'Couldn't we try to get it going?' he suggested excitedly to Gillian. 'I'm sure it's easy really. A film show just for us. We could see it twice round.'

'Rosemary can't *eat* films,' Gillian said shortly; and Sammy decided he was rather tired of the grey rabbit. Gillian was better company when she was bouncy.

The wide windows of a restaurant reminded them all how hungry they were. There were stacked-up unwashed plates on the counter and half-eaten meals (and even they looked attractive) on some of the tables. 'I hope the army have got breakfast ready,' Drake commented as they passed on. The Clock Tower had told them it was still only half-past six, but he knew that a soldier's day starts early.

The long street, which they had known only as a bustling, noisy shopping centre, packed with cars and buses that made a crossing perilous, was as lifeless as on a Sunday morning. What made it uncannily, even frighteningly, lifeless were the unlocked doors of the shops. The last person to leave a men's clothing store had been in such a hurry that he had not closed the doors behind him. Even Drake could not resist peering inside, feeling like a trespasser, to glance along the packed shelves of shirts and underclothes, the rows of hats in glass-fronted cupboards, the mahogany wardrobes with rows upon rows of hanging suits.

Gillian darted forward from behind him and ran up to an immaculately dressed dummy in city overcoat and bowler hat. With her free hand she seized the cold stiff fingers. 'How *do* you do,' she addressed the smiling figure mockingly above Drake's cries of protest. 'I'm so glad you decided to stay. Brighton is *so* bracing!'

It was not until they were in the Old Steine gardens, while Gillian was on her knees watching Rosemary nibbling furiously at the grass and Sammy was exploring the interesting emptiness of the extinguished fountain, that Drake slowly and with a growing chill at the pit of his empty stomach, realized that they might be even more alone in the big town than they had thought.

The marks of the departed tank that yesterday had stood like an ugly memorial among the flower beds, gave him the first clue. Then he saw that not only were there none of the familiar uniformed figures strolling about or on guard in the Old Steine, but that stout planks of wood had been secured across the entrance to their headquarters in the Royal Albion Hotel.

Without a word to the other two, he made his way across to the entrance to the Palace Pier and looked

The street was lifeless

carefully up and down the sea front. No one was in sight. No armoured cars patrolled the Madeira Drive, no dispatch riders tore about on motor-bicycles, and the gunposts set up on the esplanade above the beach were no longer manned and lacked their weapons.

The army had left in a body overnight, gone, perhaps, now that the invasion had taken place farther along the coast, to reinforce the defending troops. Even the sounds of battle seemed to have fallen to a distant deep boom, little louder than that of the rollers beating against the shore, and the low scudding clouds blotted out the sea and sky. It appeared likely that they were the only living people remaining in a town that had been deserted by its defenders and its inhabitants, and side-stepped by the enemy.

Drake stood for a moment in the drifting drizzle trying to take a detached view of their situation; attempting, as if from a celestial viewpoint, to see the three small figures of Sammy, Gillian, and himself in the middle of this town normally inhabited by 150,000 people. But the picture lacked clarity and he could not focus it. All he could take in was the stern fact that he had responsibilities and that there were decisions to be made.

He rejoined Sammy and Gillian in the trolley-bus shelter, where, protected from the rain and

71

with Rosemary hopping contentedly on a beautiful diamond-shaped lawn marked 'Keep off the Grass', he explained their position. They listened in silence, their eyes on his small, serious face, appearing to be giving attention while their minds raced ahead, full of plans and conjecture.

'I don't think it'll be more than a few days before everyone will be back again,' Drake told them. 'The days of trench warfare and long battles are over. Either the army will push the Germans back into the sea, or we'll retreat inland. And I'm sure we'll win. But it's no use trying to get to London now. We'll have to stay here and look after ourselves.'

'Where shall we stay?' Sammy asked suddenly. He had collected a neat stack of used trolley-bus tickets from the seats and floor of the shelter, a thing he had always been too shy to do under the gaze of waiting passengers. 'I know – let's stay at the Grand or the Metropole. We'll have huge bedrooms all to ourselves, with private bathrooms.'

As his imagination pictured those huge, wide, deep-carpeted hotel corridors, the potted plants in the great ballrooms, the hundreds of tables laid out in the dining-rooms, the lifts (oh, the time they could have with those!) he forgot his tickets in his excitement, and the words came tumbling out.

'We could cook ourselves marvellous meals in those glistening kitchens. We could go to the pictures in the morning! Stay all day if we wanted. . . .'

'And go and look into everybody's houses,' Gillian broke in, suddenly infected with Sammy's enthusiasm. She leapt on to one of the seats. 'We could explore the Foulshams' house. Think of that! We could go and look at all their father's pictures, and see what he really paints all the time.'

'And –'

'Now don't be idiots,' Drake interrupted them firmly. 'We're not breaking into anything or going anywhere we're not allowed in ordinarily. We can't go about trespassing or poking our noses into other people's houses just because there's no one here to stop us. Now pull yourselves together.'

Gillian glanced at his taut, severe face and wished all this had happened a year before, when Drake still had some fun left in him. Really, it was like being in a school instead of a family sometimes. 'And what about food?' she asked sulkily. 'I suppose you're going to allow us to *eat*, are you? Or shall we –'

'Yes, we'd all be better-tempered with a hot meal inside us,' Drake said less crossly as he got up and led the way out of the shelter. 'We're going to eat – and live – in the only house we've any right to break into.'

73

'You mean *our* house?' Sammy asked in surprise. It had never crossed his mind that, with all the thousands of interesting new houses they might live in, they would go back to Adelaide House. Fond though he was of his home, that did seem rather tame.

'Yes, come on,' Drake called back to them. 'I'm ravenous.'

For anyone who knew Adelaide House as well as the Hartfords, it was not a difficult place to break into. The latch of the smaller basement window could be pushed open with a piece of wire (hung up near by for just this emergency purpose), and the window could then be lifted up – and in one stepped.

'Won't be a second,' Drake called up reassuringly to Sammy and Gillian who were waiting by the front door. He felt his way on to his father's workbench, jumped to the floor and ran up the stairs to the hall.

There he paused for a moment, feeling suddenly as if he had forgotten something, or as if he had experienced this moment in time before.

There was something unreal about Drake Hartford standing uncertainly in the silent hall of his own house like this – 'Me, Drake Hartford,' his lips formed the words, 'age fourteen and two months, son of a doctor, living in Lewes Crescent, Brighton, in the summer of 1940. . . .' He looked about him, up the wide curving stairs, into the drawing-room, through the open door into the dining-room, the garden just visible beyond. All so familiar, all just as they had left it yesterday. And yet he had never felt more odd and out of place standing in any house – any complete stranger's house even – than he did now; never felt more in need of reassurance that he was not dreaming.

The reason for this strange feeling came to him in a sudden flash of perception that left him cold and uneasy. It was the emptiness: the empty square outside, the empty houses all around, the great empty town that, suddenly bereft of its warm, bustling inhabitants, was as discomfiting and as useless as some dead sea monster cast up from the Channel on to the pebbly shore. It had taken the emptiness of his own house, the familiar things all around, to make him realize just how alone they really were.

There was an impatient knocking on the door. 'Hey, what are you doing?' Gillian called through the letterbox. 'Let us in.'

Drake shook himself out of his momentary trance and undid the latch, and they came charging through the doorway, filling the house with their welcome noise. Gillian let Rosemary out into the back garden while

75

Sammy was given the job of rifling the kitchen store of tinned food.

'Get the frying-pan going,' Drake called downstairs after him. 'I'm just going to telephone London to try to get a message through to Mother and Father.' He went into the drawing-room, sat in his mother's soft, chintz-covered chair by the empty fireplace, and raised the receiver to his ear.

No sound came from the instrument. He joggled it up and down. Silence. Then he dialled O and waited for the dialling note. The line was dead; they were cut off.

Slowly, thoughtfully, Drake replaced the telephone on its cradle, to the sound of Sammy's indignant voice coming up from the basement kitchen: 'Hey,' he was calling, 'the gas won't work. Drake, they've turned the gas off.'

Of course, he should have anticipated this. The civil engineers would have turned everything off. He called Gillian in from the garden, and together they went downstairs and joined Sammy.

'We'd better have a cold lunch, then,' Drake said. 'Doesn't matter. We'll get a coal fire going in the drawing-room later and cook up there. I suppose the electricity's off too,' and he flicked down the switch by the door. To his surprise and relief, the light came on. And that would mean that the radio would work, that they would have news again of the outside world.

The old set on the dresser quickly warmed up, and Gillian and Sammy turned round from their energetic tin-opening when the strains of light music filled the kitchen. Almost at once an announcer's voice cut into the programme. 'This is the B.B.C. Home Service,' he said. 'We are interrupting the morning concert with the latest news of the German invasion on the Sussex coast, which began yesterday at noon.'

Sammy had the corned beef almost out of its tin; Gillian was licking spilt pineapple juice from her fingers; while Drake stood with both hands on the dresser, his head down and tilted in concentration, waiting.

But they were able to catch only three words more – 'The German army . . .' – before the voice began to fade and was swallowed up in a medley of squeals and howls. Drake frenziedly shook the little bakelite cabinet, switched the set off and on again, calling out, 'Oh, why does the thing have to break down now!'

'It isn't its fault,' Sammy said, speaking a good deal more calmly than his brother. 'Look at the light.'

He was right. The lamp had already faded to a deep yellow, dimmed rapidly to orange, and then remained this colour long enough for Gillian to climb on to the table and gaze at it in fascinated close-up. 'It's still alive,' she kept saying every few seconds, bending closer and closer to the tiny pin-point of light. 'Still there, just a flicker....'

They were all holding their breath, like a trio of naturalists brooding over the last moments of an animal whose death would mean the extinction of its breed.

'Gone!' Gillian relaxed and turned with a smile almost of relief to Drake's anxious face. 'It's all right,' she said cheerfully, leaping to the floor. 'I know where there's millions of candles.'

In the afternoon the rain turned to a fine drizzle. With his back to the fire they had lit in the drawing-room (to brighten the house up and cook on, not because they were cold), Drake said, 'I don't think there's any harm in going up on the cliffs. We might be able to see something from there.'

He looks just like Daddy when he's got something serious to say, Gillian was thinking; hands clasped behind his back, reaching up on to his toes as he talks. 'Old before his time,' she said to herself. Aloud, she said, 'Well, you don't think we're going to be cooped up here all day, do you? We're not *prisoners*.'

They were all feeling a little cross and flat. The water had failed while they were washing up, the flow of the tap dwindling first to a trickle, and then to nothing but a few drips. They would have to rely on the emergency water tanks the auxiliary fire service had placed around the town, boiling their drinking water on the fire. Many tedious discomforts loomed before them.

Sammy ran upstairs to get his *Jane's Fighting Ships*, just in case, as he explained, they caught sight of any really difficult German ships requiring identification. Then they left the house together in their raincoats, out into the chill drizzle and silence of Lewes Crescent.

The deserted trenches and gun emplacements, the abandoned armoured car which the army had evidently failed to start, made the cliff-tops look like a battlefield from which the enemy had fled. There were pools of rainwater in the trenches, and the rain had left damp beads glistening on the barbed wire like dew-soaked spiders' webs.

They walked to the edge of the cliffs and looked out over the sea. 'We shan't see much in this,' Drake said. 'Almost a fog.'

The rain clouds had fallen so low that they were standing in a fine mist that swirled about them, reducing visibility to a few hundred yards and muffling the sounds of the gunfire to the east and of aircraft flying high above them. Far below they could just make out the white splash of waves breaking on the pebbly shore.

'Do you think we're winning?' Sammy asked. He was having difficulty in wiping his soaked spectacles, and at the same time trying to protect his precious *Jane's* tucked under his raincoat.

'It's difficult to tell whether the gunfire's from farther inland or not,' Drake said slowly. 'At least this weather's stopping the Germans from using their dive-bombers. The soldiers I used to talk to up here said they hated those Stukas. They'd seen enough of them in France.'

Balancing precariously on the top of a high concrete wall, Gillian said, 'Why don't we go and see?'

'See what?' Sammy asked.

'The battle of course. We needn't actually go into the middle of it. Our bikes are in the cellar, and we could go over on them and just watch from a distance, you know.'

Drake turned and strode off towards home. 'Don't be an ass, Gillian,' he said with a short, but not unkind, laugh. 'Come on, we've got a new life to organize for ourselves – water to fetch, food to cook for supper.'

'Oh, all right,' she said, and jumped down on to the springy turf beside him. 'But I'm going to keep Rosemary in my bedroom. Nobody's going to stop me doing that. I'm not going to have her helplessly exposed to the dangers of bombing,' she added firmly, pleased with the way the right-sounding words had come to her lips.

With the coming of darkness, Adelaide House assumed a strange aspect and an atmosphere which made them all feel slightly uneasy. None of them was afraid, and even Drake managed to throw off the awful feeling of loneliness and sense of isolation which had first struck him in the hall in the morning. But, though they said nothing at first, they were all conscious of the *wrongness* of their house without the presence of their mother and father and its normal amenities of light and heat and water. They might almost have been in one of those demonstration houses put up for inspection in exhibitions; a hollow shell of a house without any soul.

And yet it was their house, their Adelaide House in which they had always lived, and it was the same as it had always been.

As if to make up for these slightly unfriendly thoughts, they found themselves being unusually polite to one another and unusually neat in their habits. Drake had developed a sense of tidiness recently anyway, but Sammy's forgetful untidiness and Gillian's rough, careless untidiness appeared to be cured in a few hours.

Mrs Hartford would have been astonished to see the meticulous manner in which Gillian and Sammy, working together with the utmost goodwill, had made up their stripped beds before tea, tucking in the sheets, folding back the tops as hospital nurses did them.

They had all been sitting in silence in the drawing-room since supper – which in itself seemed odd, for they would normally be in their rooms or the nursery at this hour. By the light of four candles stuck on to saucers, Gillian was drawing huge rather bad pictures of ponies on some drawer-lining paper she had found; Drake was making notes from his biology book – a holiday task which was no task at all; and Sammy was painting an authentic grey one of the model waterline battleships he constructed most delicately to a scale of a hundred feet to an inch.

Suddenly Sammy paused in his work, and with the paint brush poised like a wand in his fingers, looked slowly round the room.

'It's funny to think we're by ourselves, isn't it,' he said. 'I mean Mummy and Daddy not coming home, and –' he ended lamely, suddenly anxious that Drake and Gillian might think he was upset.

Drake looked up from his book with a smile. He was sitting in his father's chair, his feet upon a footstool just as Dr Hartford always sat in the evening. His father's pipe, clenched between his teeth, would not have looked odd, Gillian had decided.

'Yes, it is queer,' he said. 'We'll have to get used to things being queer for a bit.' He stood up and stretched. 'Come on, an after-dinner constitutional is what we need. Baked beans and baked beans lie heavily, I find.'

It was dark and quite silent except for the washing of the waves on the shore. The wind had veered to the west and, though they could see the narrow white fingers of search-lights probing the sky above the Newhaven area, and the sparkles of exploding anti-aircraft fire below the high cloud, the sounds of battle had faded away for the first time in thirty-six hours. Although the ground shuddered as if from a distant earthquake, it was hard to believe that thousands of soldiers were locked in combat such a short distance away.

'We'll go along to the Old Steine,' Drake said. 'We'll never have the chance of seeing it like this again.' This is what it would be like at the end of the world, he was thinking, these vibrations the dying tremors of the earthquake that has destroyed all human life – all except the three of us. The rebuilding of humanity is in our hands. . . . He had once read a story in which the whole world had been devastated by a deadly plague, leaving a group of four people who by chance came together and –

'Hey, look, there's a light on the pier!' Drake's dreaming was shattered by Sammy's excited cry. He had been walking ahead along the Marine Parade, and had halted, a small figure in the darkness, one arm pointing over the railings.

Drake and Gillian ran up and stood beside him. 'So there is,' Drake said in amazement. There had not been a light on the pier since the war had begun nearly twelve months before. On summer nights it used to be lit up by fairy lights from end to end, with a brilliant neon sign flashing out Welcome to Brighton. The side-shows, the Palace of Fun, the theatre had all been a blaze of light to lure holiday-makers. But with the black-out that had extinguished every light in Britain that might guide enemy planes, the Palace Pier had lain dark and deserted at night, a sad, abandoned playground.

More lights sprang out from the sea as they watched, first a string of hundreds of red, white, and blue fairy lights that encompassed and formed the shape of the Palace of Fun half-way along the pier; and then the illuminated ball that rotated slowly above it, flashing brilliant shafts from its mirrors like a giant sparkling diamond.

They were all too bewildered to speak for a few seconds. Who on earth could it be? Had some freak short-circuit in the town's electricity caused them to go on spontaneously? Or had the Germans already won the war, Drake wondered for a wild moment, and were celebrating their victory? And then he remembered that once, long ago, his father had for some reason told him that the Palace Pier had its own independent electricity supplied from a power plant. That would at least account for these lights when the cables in the town were dead. But who could have switched them on?

'Ssh – be quiet!' Sammy suddenly exclaimed urgently, although Drake and Gillian were still too bewildered to speak.

Then, quite clearly, they all heard the sound of a dance tune, the familiar melody of 'Roll out the Barrel', carried across the water on the westerly breeze from the pier.

There must be somebody there.

'But who on earth can it be?' Gillian asked.

'Some dotty person who refused to be evacuated yesterday,' said Drake doubtfully. 'Managed to get on to the pier somehow, though it's been barred-up since the invasion scare. And he's having a party – all by his dotty self.' He almost succeeded in frightening himself with his own theory.

'Well, we've got to find out,' Gillian said emphatically. 'Come on.' And the other two followed at a trot behind her. She was right, Drake was thinking; we've got to get to the bottom of this.

By the time they were above the Aquarium, with two or three hundred yards still to go, more lights had sprung up, 'Roll out the Barrel' had given way to a waltz, and they could hear the sound of excited shouts and of voices calling to one another.

At the Aquarium entrance they paused uncertainly, looking across the wide roundabout, where the Marine Parade and Madeira Drive met the Old Steine, to the pier entrance. Beyond the thick barbed-wire barrier that cut off all access on to the pier, they could just make out the twin ticket offices beside the turnstiles, the double gates beneath the entrance roof, surmounted by the clock tower.

Suddenly the light in the clock face and more lights above the turnstiles flashed on, and at the same time a cheer went up from the pier. 'That's better – now we can see what we're doing,' a voice cried out – the boisterous voice of a child unrestrained by the presence of grown-ups; and a voice that was horribly familiar to Drake, Gillian, and Sammy.

They could see figures moving about now, dark shapes darting about between the turnstiles and racing up and down the pier promenade beyond.

'It's – it's the Foulshams,' Sammy said quietly.

'Of course it's them,' Drake snapped, more cross with himself for being so anxious than with Sammy for stating the obvious. 'They must have missed the train, too. I wonder how on earth they got on the pier. Idiots! Putting all the lights on like that – they must be out of their minds.'

He turned round and started back for home, angry with the Foulshams for breaking the strict war-time regulation that prohibited the exposure of any light that might guide enemy aircraft; angry that he had been fooled into believing that they were alone in the town when these noisy Foulshams had been here all the time; angry that the Foulshams were taking things in their usual careless, happy-go-lucky manner – and angry that they would now have to lie low to avoid meeting them.

'Don't let's waste any time here,' he called back to Gillian and Sammy. 'Gillian, what on earth are you doing?' he shouted. The stupid girl – she'd be seen.

Gillian was running across the esplanade, was already within the area of light cast out by the clock tower and the pier lamps. Drake saw her go right up to the barbed-wire barrier and stop there with her hands on her hips.

'Where's Kensington? Where's my white rabbit?' Her voice rose, clear and insistent, above the sound of breaking rollers and the dance music from the loudspeaker farther out on the pier. 'Where's the rabbit you stole from me yesterday?' She seemed to have identified Eleanor Foulsham in the crowd of brothers and sisters milling about among the turnstiles. 'Where is she now? Have you let her loose?'

Her last words were drowned by shrieks of laughter and catcalls. One of the children was making a terrible clatter by spinning a turnstile round and round at a great rate; and Arthur had managed to climb half-way up the clock tower where he was scratching his chest with one hand and making chimpanzee cries. When he caught sight of Drake and Sammy running across the esplanade to join Gillian at the barrier, he broke off to call out to the others, 'Look, they're all here. Welcome, horrid Hartfords, fellow wanderers in a deserted city. Come and make whoopee on the pier – if you can get in.'

'Turn those lights out, you fools,' Drake called back. 'You'll have the whole German air force over here.'

'Nonsense – we're the last outpost of civilization against the Teutonic onslaught.' Arthur's reply was followed by hoots of laughter from the assembled Foulshams below. 'When the Huns come we shall die to the last man, with stiff upper lips, and backs to the wall, rather than give up. We've twenty dodgem cars as an armoured brigade – and you should see our rate of artillery fire. Fifty toffee apples a minute – nice old squashy ones that explode on impact.'

What could you do with this wild crowd of shrieking idiots, dancing about like demented Red Indians? Drake asked himself. It seemed hopeless. They could stand there for hours hurling insults at one another, but they always came off worse in a shouting match simply because they were outnumbered eight to three. This had happened so often before, always leaving Drake with a sense of lost dignity. The difference this time was that they were prevented, by the rolls of barbed wire, from attacking one another physically.

Drake took Gillian by the arm and tried to lead her away. 'Let's go home,' he said, 'we're wasting –'

'No,' Gillian answered firmly. 'I want to know what's happened to Kensington.' Eleanor Foulsham's plump, freckled face was barely ten feet away, grinning at her through the barbed wire. 'What have you done with my rabbit?' Gillian demanded again.

'You mean Van Gogh – the rabbit you stole out of our garden? I don't see that it's any business of yours, but I've got him here – safe and sound.'

'But you can't keep a rabbit on a pier. There's nowhere for her to run. Anyway, what are you feeding her on? You haven't got any grass.'

All the Foulshams were shouting or laughing and Arthur was being a chimpanzee again, screaming and bellowing above them, so that Gillian could only just

89

make out Eleanor's reply. 'Rabbits don't need exercise,' she shouted between cupped hands, while Simon, Rosetti, and Jeremy Foulsham did a war dance alongside her and made hideous faces through the barbed wire. 'I've got him in a box – and we feed him on candy floss and chocolate and sweets from the slot machines. He eats the same food as us – a well-balanced diet,' she added mockingly.

Gillian could barely control herself. 'You filthy cruel beast – you . . .' Sticky candy floss for her beloved Kensington! This was more than she could bear. She was crying hot, angry tears, sobbing with rage, when Drake at last managed to persuade her to leave.

The three of them made their way at a fast walk back across the esplanade. When they were out of sight of the pier entrance they could still hear the shrieks and cries of the children, the loud, uninhibited laughter, the voices rising unrestrainedly one above the other.

Half-way up the slope of the Madeira Drive, Drake, Gillian, and Sammy stopped for a moment and looked back at the pier below them, a long, bejewelled arm stretching out into the sea. All the fairy lights had now been switched on, and they outlined the shape of the domed Palace of Fun and every miniature minaret and archway and promenade from one end of the pier to the other. The big globe flashed out in the darkness, its light reflecting on the waves rolling in to the shore. Far out near the pier-head the arc lights on the dodgem track had been switched on, and they could see two of the cars racing wildly round and round in pursuit of one another.

Gillian stared silently at the scene of weird gaiety, thinking of Kensington cooped up in a small box, tucked away, neglected, in some corner of one of the amusement arcades; and her feeling of frustrated outrage at this cruelty was like a hard knot in her stomach.

'Drake,' she said bitterly, 'we've got to rescue her.'

Drake could understand how she felt. He used to keep pet animals himself (guinea-pigs and hamsters and white mice), and if his attitude to them had been less personal than Gillian's, he hated cruelty as much as she did. And Gillian didn't cry easily; it was a long time since he had seen her cry.

He was desperately anxious to do the right thing, to carry out his duties as temporary guardian to his brother and sister. He now had a new responsibility to face. 'To do the right thing, the right thing – but what is the right thing?' he kept asking himself.

He glanced sideways at Gillian's tear-stained face and saw her staring in angry silence at the distant figures dancing and running about on the pier promenades below.

'We'll get Kensington back,' Drake said, in a calm, ordinary voice. 'We'll go home now and work out a plan.'

5

A Question of Momentum

GILLIAN lifted the kettle off the drawing-room fire, poured the boiling water into the coffee pot, scooped Rosemary off the sofa where she was happily nibbling a carrot, and left the room with the rabbit under one arm, the steaming coffee pot in the other hand.

It was a clear sunny morning and they had decided to have breakfast on the front steps. Drake and Sammy were sitting there waiting for her, bowls of porridge on their knees.

'I think we ought to lay siege to them – starve them out,' she said as she poured out three cups of black coffee.

There was porridge for Rosemary, too; uncooked porridge oats from an elegant Wedgwood bowl: a rare delicacy in a dainty receptacle, after a night spent on the white wool hearthrug in Gillian's bedroom. Never had a rabbit enjoyed such lush living, though she remained apparently unimpressed.

'What's the use of that?' Sammy asked from the bottom step. 'If you starve them you'll starve Kensington, too.'

'We'll pass a ration of grass over the barrier every day,' Gillian said. 'That's easy. I'm going to do that this morning anyway. Candy floss!' she exclaimed in disgust again. 'Only barbarians' – she spat the word out – 'would feed a rabbit on candy floss.'

Drake looked across the empty gardens of the square to the yellow-painted house opposite. Why had the Foulshams chosen to take up residence on the pier, he wondered, and how on earth had they got on to it? It must be extremely uncomfortable, although he did not believe for a minute that they were living off the sweets and chocolates from the slot machines when the hotels and food shops in the town were packed with food. I suppose they sleep in the old theatre at the pier-head, he thought, in those plush velvet Edwardian seats from which once, long ago, he had watched a Christmas pantomime.

They were a peculiar lot! They seemed quite different from any other children he had ever known, at school or at home. They never made friends with anyone else and were always together, like a gang. Then he remembered the petty, cruel things the Foulshams had done to them in the past. Why *did* they hate Gillian and Sammy and him so much?

Drake had recently learnt that the best way to respond to the Foulshams' taunts and jeers was to ignore them, though this demanded self-restraint and left him with a feeling that he had come off worst in spite of the show of dignity. And now, in a moment of compassion for Gillian, he had promised to get back her white rabbit. One half of him regretted this rash commitment, while the other half savoured the challenge.

Sammy had suggested cutting through the barbed wire and making an assault at night when they would all be asleep. But there must be some means of getting through the barrier, or how else could the Foulshams have got on to the pier, for a solid barrier of barbed wire stretched all along the front. To lay siege to them might be a long and tedious business, but it seemed the only method of discovering a way of entry. They would have to come back into the town some time for food and drink. An observation post within sight of the entrance would be no use, for they would simply creep through at night. They needed both a place of concealment close to the pier and some means of illuminating the barrier during the hours of darkness. It was a real dilemma!

Drake finished his cup of bitter black coffee, thick with grounds, and looked up at the sound of aircraft engines. A formation of Blenheim bombers passed low overhead towards Newhaven. Early that morning the house had shaken with the vibration of gunfire and exploding bombs, and Sammy had spotted a flotilla of 'A' class destroyers racing up Channel to the scene of the battle. For a fleeting moment Drake perceived the strangeness of a situation in which they tussled with the problem of retrieving a kidnapped white rabbit while the country fought for its existence. Then he said with decision:

'All right, we'll starve them out. And if we're going to lay siege to the Palace Pier, we'll do the job properly. Put that rabbit in its cage, Gillian, fetch a bag of grass or whatever it is you feed the things on, and follow me.'

He was smiling, they noticed, and they recognized an excited, conspiratorial note in his voice that they had not heard for a long time. Sammy rushed indoors with the dirty dishes and Gillian scrambled to her feet with Rosemary in her arms. This was more like it, she was thinking – more like the old Drake!

'It's all a question of momentum,' Drake said. 'Now together, h-e-a-v-e.' And they all forced their shoulders against the rear of the armoured car.

Very slowly it began to move forward across the rough grass. 'Keep it up,' Drake begged in a strained voice. 'The faster she's moving the easier it'll be.'

Foot by foot they pushed the disabled machine across the cliff-top where the army had abandoned it, over the road verge and on to the smooth tarmac.

Once they were on the road it was easy. It descended steeply towards King's Cliff and the beginning of the Marine Parade, and almost at once the armoured car began to run away with them.

'Pile on to the back!' Drake shouted. He was roaring with laughter as he ran alongside the machine trying to grab the driver's door handle. 'Come back, you great brute,' Sammy and Gillian heard him cry out. They were already safely (or fairly safely) aboard, with their feet on a narrow bar at the rear, and clutching hold of the gun-barrel, that swung from side to side as the armoured car swerved about the road.

'Come on – jump for it!' they shouted at Drake. Oh, what fun! Why couldn't they always have fun like this? Gillian was thinking.

The armoured car was travelling at a speed of at least ten miles an hour, making straight towards the far kerb, when Drake managed to get a grip on the door handle and leap on to a steel ledge which acted as a running board. He looked back triumphantly from his precarious resting place. 'The iron horse is about to be mastered,' he called in triumph to Gillian. 'Watch me overcome the powerful steed.' His eyes were blazing with delight, his dark hair flying wildly.

'For goodness' sake get hold of the reins then,' Gillian shouted back. A high brick wall was looming up a few yards ahead and they were still accelerating rapidly.

Drake swung open the door, and with a nonchalant wave disappeared inside. At once the armoured car took on a steadier course, and they went racing down the hill at over twenty miles an hour, with Sammy now on the roof and Gillian clinging on to the gun-barrel with one hand, the bag of grass with the other.

It was not until they reached the Parade that they began to slow down, and they were travelling at barely walking pace by the time they reached Lewes Crescent.

Reluctantly Drake climbed out of the driving seat again. It had been an exhilarating drive and it had given him a wonderful sense of power to control the heavy machine along the road. He had not enjoyed himself so much for a long time.

'Off you get – and push,' he called out to Gillian and Sammy. 'Momentum, that's what counts, don't forget. Keep her moving and it won't be too bad, but if we let her stop now it'll be an awful business to get her going again.'

For the next few hundred yards the road was almost level and they had to work hard to keep the armoured car moving along the deserted Marine Parade. Then as the road began to slope down towards the sea front by the Aquarium, they found that the vehicle began to regain speed and that it no longer required pushing.

'We must make this a splendid arrival,' Drake said with relish. 'One they won't forget – a demonstration of power, in fact. Sammy, you get into the turret and swing the six-pounder barrel from side to side, you know, the way they do it in foreign countries when the army's called out to suppress riots. And you come in here with me,' he told Gillian.

He swung back into the driving seat and began steering down the inclining Marine Parade, one foot poised over the brake pedal. Through the narrow steel slit of a windscreen he and Gillian could see over the railings to the sea shimmering below, and stretching far out into it the long white-painted pier, a confusion of minarets and domed roofs, promenades and pavilions, supported by its hundreds of iron legs thrust into the water; like a giant centipede that had decided to go for a paddle, leaving its tail as a shore anchor for safety.

Squatting beside the turret on the top of the armour-plated body, Sammy could obtain an unobstructed view of the pier. The Foulshams were still there. He could see two or three figures running along the near-side promenade, and there were more red-headed children near the clock tower at the entrance.

With a grim tight-lipped expression Lieutenant Samuel Hartford opened the destroyer's turret hatch and clambered through. Once inside the cramped, dark shell, he glanced about at the familiar pattern of gun-laying instruments and controls, and his movements were steady and precise from years of training. By peering along the barrel of the six-pounder he could see the enemy, through the aperture, sighted at last after days and nights of pursuit through heavy seas – a long line of low, grey shapes on the horizon, their funnel smoke billowing out behind them.

His destroyer was at full speed ahead, every plate of her hull shivering with the strain. Below he could hear the beat of the ship's straining turbines, from outside the turret came the wash of the sea brushing past the hull. Suddenly sparks flashed along the line of distant vessels. They had opened fire! 'Range?' Sammy demanded, acknowledged the unspoken reply, and turned one of the dials above the gun's breech. . . .

The armoured car was racing down the last steep slope of the Marine Parade towards the roundabout, the pier entrance was barely fifty yards away, when Sammy suddenly called out in a clipped, commanding voice: 'Open – FIRE!'

'Oh, shut up!' came Drake's cross voice from the driving seat. 'I said "a splendid arrival". Stop playing the fool now.'

The armoured car was doing nearly thirty when they shot past the Aquarium entrance, the only sound the whine of the broad-treaded tyres on the tarmac. Drake, fighting to bring the heavy vehicle round the sharp corner, had been planning this moment of arrival since he had first thought of borrowing the army's disabled vehicle. He stamped on the brake pedal just before mounting the kerb on to the esplanade in front of the pier entrance, swung the wheel hard round so that the tail of the car swung out with a squeal from locked wheels. Twin clouds of grey smoke streamed up from under the rear, and with an ear-splitting shriek it lurched to a halt hard alongside the barbed-wire barrier.

Gillian and Drake pushed themselves back from the dashboard against which they had been thrown by the sudden halt of the armoured car.

'See any sign of them?' Drake asked breathlessly, rubbing his bruised chest which had knocked against the steering wheel.

'Yes, there they go!' With her eyes to the observation

aperture cut into the vehicle's armour-plated side, Gillian could see two of the smaller Foulshams scurrying off down the pier, glancing behind them as they ran with expressions of terror on their faces.

'Arthur! Arthur!' they were calling. 'Arthur, look! The Germans have come!'

For some minutes after the disappearance of the small Foulshams, there was nothing more to be seen or heard.

'I expect they're looking for a white flag,' Gillian whispered. 'They'll all come marching in a body begging for mercy.'

'Keep the gun turning,' Drake called quietly to Sammy in the turret. 'Got to look as if we mean business.' And he pulled the steel windscreen tight shut.

'I can see someone,' Sammy said excitedly. 'Look, it's Arthur. The other side of that line of slot machines. He keeps putting his head out and ducking back.'

Drake clambered back into the turret beside Sammy, and peered through the gun-sighting aperture. 'Yes, there they are,' he confirmed. 'All eight of them. Huddled together like a flock of frightened sheep. Come here, Gillian, this is worth looking at.'

Gillian forced her way into the crowded turret, and the three of them watched in expectant delight to see what would happen next.

'It's really rather a shame,' Drake went on from beside her. 'They probably think we're going to mow them down like ninepins. I think it's time we ordered them off.'

'Oh no, a bit longer,' Gillian begged. 'Think of all the things they've done to us. Let's fire off one round over their heads!'

'Don't be an ass! Anyway, we'd probably blow ourselves up too. I'm going to do my stuff now.' And Drake groped his way back into the driving compartment, and half-opened one of the steel doors far enough for his voice to be heard without allowing himself to be seen.

He felt so foolish and self-conscious that several seconds passed before he could bring himself to utter the words of command, in a strong German accent. Then he took a deep breath, and in as loud and commanding a voice as he could manage, called out:

'Achtung! Achtung!

'In ze name of ze Fuehrer, we call on you to surrender. Our guns are trained on you and one shot and you will be blown up. Come out with your hands op above your heads, and leave your arms behind.'

As the last words echoed and faded inside the armoured car, Gillian and Sammy could control themselves no longer and burst into giggles.

'Be quiet!' Drake ordered, more because he was offended than because he thought the Foulshams would hear. It had been a very difficult thing to do, and he thought he had managed rather well.

They awaited developments in silence. They heard the Foulshams before they saw them. It was Arthur's voice, sounding uneasy and faintly querulous, that called out, 'All right, we're coming. We're only children, you know. We haven't got any arms, look!'

And there he was, standing uncertainly in the centre of the promenade, his arms high above his head, one hand signalling to the others to follow him from the shelter of the slot machines.

'Kom, kom – schnell!' Drake ordered, growing more confident with every word. 'We haf no time to waste and the German navy it needs this pier.'

In single file all eight Foulshams walked in step, in descending order of size, down the wooden-slatted promenade towards the entrance: eight red heads, eight frightened white faces. Through the turnstile they came, pausing in turn to rotate the iron spokes awkwardly with their bodies – clack, clack, clack! – then continuing their advance towards the barbed wire.

'Talk about the goose-step,' Gillian giggled, 'it's more like Duck's Ditty.'

'Pit pat paddle pat, pit pat waddle pat,' Sammy whispered, now firmly back in the world of reality.

'Now line up in a row,' Drake's voice boomed out

again, 'and you – you big boy at ze end. Open op ze barrier and kom out.'

Oh, but this was almost worth the loss even of Kensington, Gillian was thinking. This was a sight she would never forget. And anyway in a few minutes they would all be on the pier to rescue her. . . .

In a few minutes! But within seconds from the moment when Arthur Foulsham must have revealed how they had got through the barbed wire, they saw Eleanor suddenly drop one arm and catch hold of her brother's sleeve. She was whispering excitedly in his ear and pointing at the armoured car.

'Schnell! Schnell!' Drake repeated nervously when he noticed these suspicious moves. 'And keep your hands op – all of you, or we fire!'

But it was no use. One by one, until only Simon's short arms were raised, the Foulshams' hands fell to their sides, and like a dismissed class they broke up into their familiar jostling mêlée.

'It's only the horrid Hartfords!' Eleanor shrieked. 'It's all right – it's only a joke. It's not a German armoured car at all.'

'Look at the tyres – they're Dunlops,' Arthur added his deeper voice to the outburst of shouting from all his brothers and sisters. 'Who ever heard of a German armoured car with English tyres?'

Drake was prepared for this eventuality and called back to Gillian, 'The bluff's called. Up you go.'

Gillian reached up, swung back the steel hatch and climbed out on to the roof. A chorus of howls and jeers greeted her from the massed Foulshams dancing and waving their arms below. But for once she remained unaffected; she had tasted triumph more satisfying than any exchange of blows could give. If their ruse had only partly worked, it had been worthwhile just to see the foolish Foulshams really made to look foolish.

Standing beside the muzzle of the six-pounder gun with her hands on her hips, she waited for a lull in the tumult, and then called out in a clear voice, 'All right then, we're not Germans. But you looked jolly silly lined up there like a – And it doesn't alter the fact,' she continued, raising her voice above the rising boos and hisses, 'that this *is* an armoured car and we're at the right end of a machine-gun and a six-pounder. And we're staying here, we're going to starve you out until –'

But the rest of her speech was lost in the catcalls and shouts from the angry children. 'We've food to last for weeks,' she heard Arthur's deeper voice cry out. 'We've got *batteries* of anti-tank guns.'

Gillian jumped down on to the pavement and took the bag of grass from Drake's outstretched hand. 'Don't mind their ragging,' he told her as he passed it over.

This was a sight she would never forget.

'We've won a terrific moral victory, and they know it. Just be dignified.'

'I'll freeze them with my cold stare,' Gillian answered with a laugh. 'Just you watch.'

Swinging the bag at her side she strolled across the few yards that separated her from the barrier as if she were going shopping.

Eleanor Foulsham came forward to greet her, making a series of outrageous faces and then crouching down to glare at her through the barbed wire. Gillian had to admit that she had got over her moment of fear with remarkable speed; and she tossed over the bag, which landed at Eleanor's feet. 'The only person we're allowing to eat – until you give her back – is my rabbit,' she told her coldly. 'The rest of you are starving.'

Eleanor picked up the bag and pushed her face inside like a horse with a nose-bag of chaff. When she withdrew it there were grass clippings all over her chubby face and she was hooting with affected laugher. 'Hey, look at this,' she called to Arthur. 'Food for Van Gogh.' She swung back to Gillian with bared teeth. 'Food to fatten him up – so that he's worth EATING,' she yelled triumphantly, rotating her lower jaw and poking her fingers into her mouth as if savouring tender morsels.

Then she suddenly leapt up from her squatting position and ran back with weird cries through the turnstiles, down the pier promenade, and with a last shout of 'Rabbits like candy floss best, food for the fishes!' hurled the bag into the sea.

Gillian only just managed to suppress an outburst of protest at this new demonstration of cruelty. But remembering Drake's careful briefing a few minutes before and when they had made their preparations earlier in the morning, she turned away from the leaping, dancing, mocking crowd of Foulshams and, pale with anger, walked back to the armoured car.

'Did you hear what she said?' she asked Drake in an outraged voice when she was inside the car again. 'Honestly, I think they *would* kill her and –'

'Now don't be silly,' Drake answered soothingly. 'Don't you see, they're only trying to make you rise. They don't mean a word of it.'

'But how are they going to feed Kensington?' Gillian demanded, near to tears. 'Did you see what they did with the grass?'

'Yes, yes,' Drake said, trying to reassure her, although his voice carried little conviction. 'But I expect she only did that because they've got a store of rabbit food. Sammy,' he said, turning to his brother, who had been silently contemplating the antics of the Foulshams through the aperture, 'you and Gillian go and get some lunch now. I'll take first watch, till six o'clock. You can bring me down something to eat if you like. Then Gillian can take over for the first night watch.' And he opened the off-side door to let them out.

Gillian and Sammy had almost reached Lewes Crescent when they heard the sudden rattle of machine-gun fire from the sea sounding clear above the boom of battle which now seemed to have become a permanent background noise which they no longer noticed. Together they raced to the railings overlooking the Madeira Drive and the shore.

'They've attacked him – they've attacked him already,' Sammy said excitedly. 'That was Drake firing. We'll have to go to the rescue.'

'I can't see any smoke,' Gillian said, staring at the distant pier. 'And look, they're still playing on the dodgems.' She could just make out three little cars racing round and round the track. They would hardly be likely to attack Drake lacking three of their number.

Then there was another burst of fire, louder and longer than the last, and Gillian and Sammy realized this time that it came from a point far east of the Palace Pier – from a fighter plane streaking close behind a fleeing bomber some two miles out at sea. Together the two jinking, swerving machines raced towards Rottingdean, one following every move of the other as if it were its shadow, rose up over the cliffs and disappeared.

'Oh, it's only an aeroplane,' Gillian said in disgust. 'Come on, I'm hungry after all that pushing.' And even Sammy, who had never been interested in the air and had, in any case, seen many dog-fights during the past two days, felt that he had been let down.

'What'll we have?' he asked. 'I'm getting fed up with baked beans.'

6

A Question of Courage

B Y FOUR o'clock Drake was so bored and uncomfortable that he was ready to throw in his hand and withdraw from the siege. As the afternoon dragged on and the steel roof of the armoured car, on which he was sunning himself with his shirt off, became harder and harder, the belief that he – a fourteen-year-old approaching man's estate – was really past this childish nonsense began to take root in his mind.

And the idea that Gillian and Sammy should stand watch in turns through the night was so absurd that he could not imagine how he had ever come to suggest it.

Since two o'clock there had been no sign of movement on the silent pier. Several church clocks in the town rang out the hour in turn; Drake had now learnt to identify them and the order in which they chimed, some overlapping others, and one, far away towards Hove, ringing at a longer and longer interval after the rest at each quarter-hour. Perhaps it was already running down. In a few days all the clocks would be silent, and Brighton would seem more dead than ever. The whole town was running down, dying cell by cell, like animals on a deserted farm. Already the food left behind in the shops would be going bad. Rust and rot would set in; the damp would slowly creep into the houses and hotels, the shops and offices. In another few weeks the leaves would start to fall, clogging the gutters and drains....

But everyone will be back long before then, Drake decided, trying to reassure himself. The invasion battle would be over in another few days at the most, and the Old Steine, which he could see from the armoured car's roof, would be full again of buses and cars and the shoppers and business people and holiday-makers who used to throng the tree-shaded pavements and gardens before the war. And the term will have started, and I will be back at school, Drake was thinking....

Then the Foulshams attacked, scattering all his idle thoughts.

It was at once uncomfortably clear that they were not bluffing about the toffee apples. The stall keeper who had been bustled off the pier with all the others weeks before, when the invasion threat began with the German conquest of France, must have left his stock behind.

The Foulshams had obviously discovered the apples and recognized what perfect ammunition they would make.

The attack was well-planned and Drake was taken completely by surprise when they opened up a barrage from carefully prepared positions beyond the entrance gates to the pier. Even the signal to open fire must have been given in silence, for Drake's first knowledge of the attack came with the arrival of a storm of these over-ripe projectiles, which exploded all over the side of the armoured car with fruity thuds.

The second volley was accompanied by high-pitched war cries, and this time two of the toffee apples struck home, hitting Drake painfully on his bare chest and sending syrupy streaks across his face and the pages of the biology book he was reading.

In undignified haste he scrambled to his feet, opened up the hatch, and, as a third volley whistled overhead and splashed about him, disappeared inside – forced to agree, in confirmation of the Foulshams' triumphant cries, that he had suffered humiliating defeat.

Drake remained in a black, determined mood until Gillian turned up to relieve him at six o'clock. When he saw her running past the Aquarium entrance, waving and smiling as she always waved and smiled whenever she arrived anywhere, he felt warmed and less depressed.

Gillian had her faults as a sister, but there was no denying that her presence was nearly always cheering and exhilarating.

'Where have they all gone? Prostrated by starvation, I suppose,' Gillian greeted Drake while she still had a dozen yards to run (or skip, as the fancy took her).

Drake eased his stiff body out of the driving seat and dropped to the pavement. 'They made a full-scale assault earlier,' he told her. 'But they retired when I gave them a few short bursts with the machine-gun.'

'Did you really?' Gillian asked, her eyes blazing. 'Did you fire at them? How many did you kill?' The gullible Gillian, a certain victim of the wildest joke, glanced round the vehicle at the pier, half expecting to see piled bodies of Foulshams. 'You must show me how to work the gun,' she said seriously.

With an expression of affectionate pity on his face, Drake patted her arm and said, 'Too late for that, old girl. I've finished them all off.'

There was a short pause before Gillian turned to her brother. 'You beast,' she said. 'You're pulling my leg.'

'Never mind,' Drake said with a broad smile, 'but they really did attack, with toffee apples – which hurt, in case you don't know. So you'd better stay inside with the screens bolted down. We'll swing the machine round so that it's facing the barrier, in case you need the lights. Arthur Foulsham's not as dumb as you. He knows we wouldn't really fire on him – but he also knows that we've got an impregnable observation post, and that if they leave the pier, one of us is on duty to watch how they get through the barrier.'

'But that may not be for ages,' Gillian said with an expression of concern on her face. 'And Kensington will have starved to death by then.'

'I wouldn't worry about that,' Drake said with insufficient conviction. He began to reverse the armoured car on full lock, heaving at the front. 'Come on, give a hand,' he told her as he strained at the heavy vehicle and slowly got it moving. 'Anyway there's nothing we can do about it until they show their hand.'

When the front of the armoured car was facing the barrier, he helped Gillian up into the driving seat. 'Now don't forget to switch the lights on when it gets dark if they don't put the pier lights on. I'll be back at midnight and we'll bring you something to eat before then. Sammy can take the early morning watch; I don't want him here by himself when it's dark.'

As Gillian watched him crossing the esplanade towards the Marine Parade she already felt the first pangs of loneliness and boredom: six long, blank hours faced her. 'Hey,' she suddenly called after him. 'Make sure

Rosemary's all right, will you? Give her some carrots – she's in the back garden.'

Drake turned and gave a brief wave of acknowledgement. Then he disappeared beyond the Aquarium, and she was alone. . . . Alone, except for the Foulshams; for no sooner was Drake out of earshot than Gillian heard Eleanor Foulsham calling to her from the other side of the barrier, and saw her through the narrow aperture standing by the wire, alone this time, looking suddenly rather small and vulnerable, a tentative smile on her round, freckled face.

'I don't know what's happening to the rabbit,' she called out to Gillian in an anxious voice. The slightest suggestion of any rabbit's distress would be certain to bring Gillian running, and at any time she was innocent of suspecting motives. She jumped down to the pavement and ran to the barrier.

'Why, what's the matter?' she asked breathlessly. She saw that Eleanor Foulsham's brow was furrowed by a perplexed frown, and that her pale blue eyes were wide with worry.

'Well, you know so much more about rabbits than I do,' Eleanor said in a soft, simpering tone. 'So I thought you might be able to advise me. I know you think Van Gogh's yours, but I thought you would agree that where the welfare of a pet animal is

117

concerned we should all help one another? Don't you think so?'

'Yes, but what's the *matter*?' Gillian asked again, impatient but still unsuspecting.

'The thing is,' Eleanor said, with maddening slowness and pausing at every word, 'that candy floss isn't suiting him very well, just as you thought. He's listless and vomits after every meal, and he's getting terribly thin and –'

'And he's hardly going to make a square meal for two of us, let alone eight.'

Gillian swung towards the sound of the voice of Arthur, who had sidled up quietly. She saw the expression of mock distress on his face, and heard at the same moment Eleanor's sudden roar of malicious laughter.

As she turned from one mocking face to the other, Gillian was so appalled and overcome at the cruel joke that she could do nothing but stare at them in openmouthed horror. 'Oh, you – you, you – how can you –?' But the words of outrage were suffocated by the torrent of anger that swept over her. It was too much, too much for anyone to bear. . . .

Unconscious of what she was doing, unaware even of the hot tears falling over her cheeks, she turned with head lowered and walked slowly back to the armoured car. She did not hear Arthur's word of command to his three brothers, who had been waiting with fire extinguishers, taken from their brackets in the pier theatre; did not see them suddenly charge up to the barrier, press the extinguishers' firing mechanisms, and swing the nozzles in her direction. And she was so lost in her cloud of misery and anger that at first she hardly felt the hard jets of liquid stinging against her back. The raucous yells and jeers that accompanied the onslaught were no worse than the recurrence of an old familiar pain, a pain that was dulled by comparison with the sharp, stabbing agony of fear for her white rabbit, starving and facing a death which it appeared impossible for her to prevent.

Those hours of despair and bitterness between six o'clock and nightfall would have scarred for life any girl less bouncy and ebullient than Gillian. But when Drake asked her several days later what she did after the fire-extinguisher attack, she only answered after a moment's deep thought, 'Plotted, I suppose – plotted how I could rescue Kensington.'

She had by then forgotten the black agony of that evening when she had sat huddled in the stuffy, steel-encased driving cab of the armoured car, her sodden, clothes sticking clammily to her skin, thinking in turn of the pain and suffering Kensington must be enduring, of ways of getting her back again (each seeming more impossible than the last), and, less charitably, of how much she hated the cruel, thoughtless gang of Foulshams, for whom death by slow torture would have been an undeserved kindness.

Slowly the sun swung lower and lower over the sea, disappearing at last behind the Royal Albion Hotel. And with the first chill of twilight, Gillian's mind was made up. She was unaccustomed to indecision and was unable any longer to bear the prospect of spending another three hours idly plotting and nursing her sour-tasting hatred.

It did not in the least matter that it was a wild plan, with the smallest chance of success and every chance of resulting in her serious injury.

She said nothing to Drake and Sammy when they turned up with her supper and stayed for a few minutes to see that everything was all right before going back to the house for some sleep. Her mind was made up, and she did not even dare to mention the Foulshams' last attack in case Drake should insist on her going back to change into dry clothes.

'Better put the lights on now,' Drake told her as he left. 'Pinch yourself every ten seconds to keep yourself awake,' he added with a laugh. 'I'll be back at midnight. Not scared, are you?'

'Scared? Of that gang of idiots? Don't be such an ass.' What an idea! And she slammed the door shut and settled herself back in the driving seat with her arms folded, her eyes gazing along the thin beams of the hooded headlamps, shining on to the barbed-wire barrier.

She would wait another half-hour, not a moment longer. Her only anxiety was that the Foulshams might switch on the fairy lights about the entrance, and the clock light above, for it was essential that she should be able to leave the armoured car unobserved; but so far they had illuminated only the far end of the pier, from which occasional high-pitched shrieks of excitement reached her.

From the top of the steps leading down from the esplanade to the beach, Gillian glanced back for the last time to the barricaded pier entrance lit up by the shafts of light from the headlamps of the armoured car standing like some bulky primeval beast glaring at its foe. Then she ducked down under a board saying THE BEACH IS A PROHIBITED AREA BEWARE OF MINES, and set about her first obstacle.

It was only a single roll of barbed wire, like a loosely-bound cocoon, designed rather to discourage residents from venturing on to the beach than to prevent invading Germans from coming ashore. She had tackled these before, for Brighton front had been fortified for weeks and she had often found it necessary to break into forbidden areas. By stretching wide the strands and easing herself into the network head first like a snake piercing a thick bramble hedge, she managed to force her way through with no more damage than a cut finger and three long tears in her shirt.

Below her, half-way down the steps, there was a more formidable triple barrier of wire. In daylight she had seen that this could be avoided by taking a chance on a drop on to the concrete lower promenade, a high enough fall when the distance could be judged, but in the darkness it might as well have been (as Jules Verne would have described it) a bottomless gulf. Even Gillian, who had spent a good part of her life falling and rolling, jumping and tumbling, hesitated momentarily with her legs dangling over the edge of the stone balustrade.

Then she pushed herself off into the darkness and fell and fell – and at last struck the unresisting promenade, the soles of her feet stinging and her whole body shaken by the sudden jar.

Gillian raised herself painfully from the concrete and looked up at the high pier above her. Seen from underneath it was no longer a bright, frivolous playground, but a dark, skeleton framework of crisscrossed cast iron, a giant, complex bridge reaching out from the esplanade, over the lower promenade on which Gillian was standing; over the narrow strip of pebbly beach, and far out over the waves: a bridge over the sea leading to nowhere.

There was something mysterious in this curious dark world beneath the pier that added a sinister touch to the challenge she had to face. Here the pebbles crunched hollowly underfoot and the surf broke with a deeper boom on to the shore; and an odour of stale seaweed and decaying fish hung in the air.

Gillian looked up into the faintly outlined tracery of pillars and diagonal cross-struts, seeking out the best place from which to begin the long climb. Then she reached up, gripped a narrow girder and swung her legs out. . . .

It was easier now that she had started, and the little flicker of fear she had felt died to nothing.

To reach the point of intersection of one of the X-shaped cross-struts was not difficult. Here she paused for a moment to regain her sense of balance and allow her eyes to accustom themselves to the darkness. The next stretch up a narrow forty-five-degree bar tested her nerves more severely, for there was no hand-grip above; and half-way up she had to let her legs drop and had to climb more slowly hand over hand, her feet swinging below. When she felt her sandals grazing one of the main pillars she gripped it with her ankles as if it were a tree trunk and reached up with her hands to a projecting bolt above her head.

It was an insecure position, and a painful one, for the pillar was rusty and scraped her bare legs, but she could hold herself there just long enough to be able to peer upwards to work out her next move.

She thought that there was another bolt two or three feet higher, but she could not be certain . . . and her feet were beginning to lose their grip, sliding and tearing her skin against the rough surface. Somehow she must get higher, somehow. . . .

Pulling on her arms with all her strength she managed to raise her body very slowly, clutching the pillar with her knees every few inches to give added support. One finger touched the welcoming projection; she would be all right if she could get her hand round it. But oh, her knees! She nearly cried out with the agony.

Now she had a firm hold on the rusty bolt with her right hand, her left hand joined it, and at the same time she got her sandals on to the lower bolt. At last she was safe again, hands and feet on the conveniently spaced projections, able to stand in reasonable comfort with her body held flat against the pillar. Here she could rest her aching muscles for a moment, steady herself for the next stage and draw in deep lungfuls of the sea-soaked air.

It was not far to the top now, only another ten feet or so. By leaning her head back she could see beyond the underside of the pier promenade to the clear starry sky above, while below . . . At once she wished that she had not looked down. The beach, with the waves pounding themselves to a white death on the pebbles below, appeared terrifyingly far away.

But nothing could have broken Gillian's nerve now. She had conquered what she thought was the worst part of the climb and had nearly proved that the Foulshams' stronghold was not impregnable. Above her she could make out a cross-girder that seemed comfortably within reach, and from this it would be an easy climb to the outside of the railings bordering the promenade.

The girder was farther away than she had thought, but by stretching up on to tip-toe on the bolt she just managed to brush it with her finger-tips; and with a little spring she got her hand round it, with her legs dangling in space, away from the pillar. Now for her left hand. . . .

She let go of the bolt and reached up. And it was at this crucial moment, when she was hanging in space by one arm, that her hand slipped from the edge of the girder. It slipped slowly, inch by inch at first, so that she thought for a second that she could still save herself by finding a second hand-hold. Then with her left arm waving about helplessly in space, her legs kicking in search of the lost pillar, she realized with a sudden surge of horror that she was going to fall.

In that last despairing second before surrendering, her left hand touched an iron bar, her fingers locked round it, and as she lost the girder with her right hand, she was left dangling like a garden swing with a broken rope.

At the beginning of the climb she could have drawn her body and legs up and over that girder in one movement; but now she was tired, every muscle had been strained beyond endurance, and it took long, agonized seconds for her to gather her strength, grip the girder with both hands, and slowly, painfully draw herself up by bending her arm. She rested for a moment with her chest on the hard iron, then pulled her legs over in turn and sat astride the girder, panting so hard that she thought she would be sick.

She had won. She had never before been so near to a fall that might have killed her, and when the trembling that shook her body subsided, she felt a wonderful sense of triumph. It was easy now. The lattice-work of girders was as close-set as the branches of a yew tree, and she was able to grope her way up without any further trouble to the pipe that ran along the underside of the pier floor. By standing on this she was able to draw herself out and up on to a ledge, swing her legs over the railings, and land on the wood-slatted pier promenade.

She was some fifty yards from the entrance, and she could see the headlamp beams from the armoured car shining through the barrier, casting a wan yellow light on the gates and the two turnstiles and the darkened clock tower. All was still and silent at that end of the pier. But the head of the pier was still brightly illuminated and she could hear the whine of the dodgem cars and the cries of the Foulshams. Did they never go to bed? Gillian wondered. It was already nearly eleven o'clock. Not that she cared, for the harder they played and the more noise they made, the better chance it gave her of finding Kensington.

Keeping close to the shelter that ran down the centre of the pier, she made her way towards the Palace of Fun and looked through one of the glass doors. There were lights on in the big domed-roof pavilion, but only one Foulsham was visible in the forest of slot machines and empty stalls. It was the eight-year-old Vincent, who was engaged in a hectic game of pin-football with himself, operating both handles and uttering cries of encouragement to both teams simultaneously as the ball flicked from end to end of the pitch. When he had finished, Gillian noticed, he took a huge bunch of keys from his trouser pocket, undid the lock below the slot, retrieved his penny, and slipped it into the fruit machine next door. So that was one way (and a cheap way) in which the Foulshams entertained themselves!

Beyond the Palace of Fun she had to be more cautious, for the pier promenades were brightly lit and there was little cover, and the sounds from the Foulshams ahead of her were louder than ever. 'Hey, Arthur, did you see me crash him? I get four points for that,' she heard Randolph Foulsham claim shrilly. 'That means I'm in the finals.' There appeared to be some sort of dodgem championship taking place.

'If I can only get past the track to the end of the pier without being seen, I'll be all right,' Gillian decided. She was certain that Kensington would be somewhere near the Foulsham headquarters, which she now knew must be in the theatre building.

But that was not going to be easy. The pier widened just ahead of her; on one side was the dodgem car track, on the other the ghost train, which seemed to be running a nonstop service manned by three of the younger Foulshams, eliminees, in all probability, from the dodgem championship. They had somehow contrived to make the train travel at three times its normal speed, and the weird-looking locomotive with its three carriages in the shapes of a coffin, an ambulance, and a hearse, was lurching in and out of the dark tunnels and back through the station again at breakneck speed, encouraged by its shouting passengers. Both the dodgem track and the ghost train station were brightly illuminated by arc lights, and Gillian's only sheltering places were scattered stalls and kiosks spaced down the centre of the pier.

Running bent double, Gillian reached the safety of an ice-cream kiosk and crouched in its shadow. A dozen yards away the ghost train came swaying out of its last tunnel (marked with a skull and crossbones and the words SCARED? FIND OUT – 6d.), charged through the platform that normally signalled the end of the sixpennyworth, and disappeared again into THE WORLD'S MOST TERRIFYING CHAMBER OF HORRORS with its load of shouting children.

This was the moment to run for the next shelter, a shooting gallery with high wooden sides. After a quick glance towards the dodgem track, Gillian darted across the short length of open promenade and leapt over the side and into the gallery. Inside it was like a pen, with a number of targets, peppered through and through by the Foulshams, and above them on shelves a large quantity of highly undesirable prizes, mostly curiously shaped vases in shades of mauve, purple, and cream.

On the wooden floor of the shooting gallery there was a scattering of grass, and Gillian was surprised to notice a half-nibbled carrot or two, a small feeding bowl. Had she by an extraordinary chance . . . Yes, there she was, poking her pink nose tentatively out of a cosy, hay-lined hutch in the corner, ears flat back from the shock of her mistress's sudden arrival.

'Kensington! My darling Kensington,' Gillian cried, and crawled on her knees, arms outstretched, towards her white rabbit. 'And they told me you were pining away on candy floss. But you look more beautiful than ever.' Beneath her hand the ears lying along Kensington's back were like strips of velvet on cotton wool. She touched her soft nose with a finger-tip, caressed the delicate whiskers and stared lovingly into the blankly unemotional eyes.

'Now how am I going to get you away? You'll have to crawl through the barbed wire – that'll be easy for you while I climb down under the pier again.' Crouched against the corner of the shooting gallery, she went on murmuring quietly to Kensington, oblivious of the recurring roar of the ghost train as it shot in and out of the tunnels, and oblivious of the sudden silence from the dodgem track.

She never saw the figure of Jeremy Foulsham come up silently behind her, failed to hear his muffled exclamation of surprise. Nor did she see Eleanor answer Jeremy's wave of command to join him. Her first clue that she had been seen was the longer shadow from Arthur, which fell across Kensington's snow-white back, and made her look up. By then there were three Foulshams lined up above her, grinning in silent triumph.

None of them uttered a word until she leapt frantically to her feet with Kensington in her arms and attempted to leap the wall of the gallery. Then with a blood-curdling whoop, they descended on her. 'A mutineer – a mutineer in our midst,' Arthur shouted. 'String her up from the highest yard-arm, keel-haul her, make her walk the plank, throw her to the sharks.' He jumped up on to the counter, grabbed one of the rifles and aimed it at the jostling crowd grappling with Gillian. 'One more move out of you,' he yelled in a poor imitation American accent, 'and I'll fill yer full of lead!'

The ghost train ground to a halt and the passengers piled out on to the platform and ran across to the shooting gallery, all shouting at the tops of their voices. The five-year-old Simon leapt down from the telescope platform ('A PENNY FOR A WONDERFUL LOOK') from which he had been studying the stars, and joined the crowd. Vincent reappeared, running down the pier clutching the chocolates he had won in the Palace of Fun in one hand, and swinging the keys in the other. The Foulsham entourage was complete, all eight of them milling about the helpless Gillian like a lynch mob, while Kensington cowered in her cage at their feet.

'Silence!' Arthur called, waving a rifle in each hand now. 'Silence, ye fruity Foulshams. A decision is to be made. This ghastly, prim, overdressed, simpering miss of a Hartford has had the temerity to invade our sacred citadel – how I know not – to attempt once again to steal the noble, handsome Van Gogh. What shall we do with her? Keel-haul her? String her up –'

'Throw her to the sharks,' came a chorus of voices from the bobbing red heads about Gillian. 'Over the side with her.'

The two rifles went off with a double explosion, Arthur leapt off the counter, and led the way over the gallery wall towards the pier edge.

Four hands seized each of Gillian's ankles, two more each of her wrists, and she was carried upside down, helplessly across the promenade and lifted on to the top of the iron railings. Far, far below she could see the fairy lights reflecting like wriggling beads of pearls in the black water. The sea was rough, it was a long drop, and then a long way to the shore. . . .

Gillian never discovered whether the younger Foulshams really would have hoisted her over the side. And they were in such a wild state of excitement that they did very nearly let her drop before she heard

Arthur suddenly call out, 'All right, we'd better give her something to keep her feet dry. Probably never been in anything deeper than a bath before. Hoist out the lifeboat, Jeremy, and I suppose she'll have to have some oars.'

So they had a boat! That was how they had first got on to the pier, and renewed their supplies (including food for Kensington) from the town. No wonder they had not taken the siege very seriously. They must somehow have found a way through the barbed-wire entanglements on to the beach, taken one of the fishermen's boats and rowed out to the landing stage at the end of the pier. Once on the pier, they had the use of a second boat, a white-painted lifeboat that was, Gillian now remembered, always kept ready for emergency use.

The lifeboat was already slung out on its davits, and Gillian was ordered into this at gun-point by Arthur, who continued to direct operations, balanced precariously on the railings. 'Don't know why we're being so soft with this mealy-mouthed mutineer, do you?' he asked the others.

'We ought to disembowel her first,' Rosetti muttered with a dreadful expression on her little freckle-covered face.

Although she had been frightened for one moment, and had been bruised by her rough treatment, Gillian was determined to show she did not care. If she had

Gillian was determined to show she did not care

found Kensington really starving and ill-treated it might have been different, but having seen that her rabbit was not dying and, to her surprise, that she was in fact well looked after, she was able to face the jeers and shouts of the Foulshams who lined the rails watching her disappear into the darkness. She had a rough passage down to the sea, Jeremy and Randolph, who were operating the davits, deliberately allowing first the stern and then the bows of the boat to drop in sudden jerks. When she was some ten feet above the waves, they cut the ropes and the boat fell with a crack into the sea, shipping water over the sides.

After being thrown by a wave against one of the pier's pillars, the lifeboat turned slowly round and began moving away east. Far above her, Gillian could see the heads of the eight children leaning over the railings, and could hear Arthur's mocking voice calling 'Bon voyage. It's only 16,000 miles to the nearest shore. If Captain Bligh could make it, so can you.'

A few toffee apples fell into the sea around her, and one crashed into the boat at her feet. Then the boat drifted out beyond the range of the pier lights, rising and falling on the swell, and turning slowly round and round.

Gillian lay back in the seat at the stern, gazing idly at the flashes and sudden explosions which were lighting up the sea towards Newhaven and Beachy Head. There was nothing she could do but wait until daylight, and hope that she would not be too seasick and would eventually come ashore. For both the lifeboat's oars had been lost during the rough descent from the pier.

7

United Forces

THE sound of Drake's footsteps on the stairs sent Sammy scurrying back into bed, and his eyes were tight shut and he had the blankets and sheets drawn up to his chin when the door opened. The torch beam flashed round the bedroom, rested for a second on his bed, and was snapped off again. He heard the door shut quietly, the footsteps recede down the two flights to the hall, and Sammy sprang to the window again in time to see Drake emerge from the front door below and disappear into the darkness of Lewes Crescent.

Sammy had been dressed in shorts and jersey for the past hour ready for this moment when he would be left alone in the house. To have only a part-view of the great naval action that had been going on far out in the Channel was more than he could endure. After all, he told himself, naval battles did not happen on your doorstep every day of your life.

He only had to slip his feet into his sandals before leaving his room and running down the dark stairs. Drake had left a candle burning in the hall and there was a pan of soup warming on the drawing-room fire for Gillian when she returned from her spell of duty. It was just after half-past eleven, and Sammy reckoned he had a full half-hour of sightseeing ahead of him.

From the railings high up on the Marine Parade, he had a grandstand view of the battle, although it was taking place a long way out to sea and it was impossible to make out what was happening. The whole of the south-eastern horizon seemed to be alight with hundreds of pin-point flashes which were broken every few seconds by sudden white glows that illuminated the sea and died again at once. Deep red spurts of flame that might have been explosions from direct hits shot up, showering sparks into the night sky, while above the line of invisible vessels the pencil-thin searchlight beams swung to and fro, paused and moved off again on their blind search. Hundreds of anti-aircraft guns sent shower after shower of tracer shells arching up, their line of flight deceptively lazy and casual, as if someone were poking the embers of a giant fire.

'I expect this'll be in the history books as the Battle

of Brighton,' Sammy told himself. 'And I can say that I saw it.' This was the spectacle he knew he would never forget.

One of the ships caught fire as he watched. He saw a gush of flame shoot up, casting a red glow on the underside of its own black funeral pyre, and half a minute later a deeper boom rose above the continuous thunder of gunfire and exploding bombs that came echoing across the water.

Then another sound reached him from the sea, the sound of a voice that, because he was so absorbed in the distant battle, repeated its cry many times before he recognized it. 'Hey, Drake!' the voice called. 'Hey, I'm here. Help!'

It was Gillian's voice all right. She was calling out from a long way away, from somewhere out beyond the line of rollers breaking on the shore. Sometimes the cry of distress was lost in a louder explosion from the battle, but Sammy was in no doubt who it was. But what on earth was she doing in the sea?

Sammy cupped his hands and shouted back at the top of his voice. 'All right, coming!' Drake could not be far away, Sammy reckoned, for he had been standing by the railings for only a few minutes.

Only fragments of Gillian's high-pitched cries of distress reached him:

'– in a boat – adrift – a boat – stuck –'

Sammy had no particular plan in mind when he began running along the pavement towards the path that led down the steep slope to the Madeira Drive below – the path on which Gillian had encountered the Foulshams on the day before the invasion. He only knew that he must, if he could, find a way through the fortifications to the beach, and somehow do something to help her.

He was about to turn down the path through the shrubbery when Drake appeared out of the darkness running towards him. 'Did you hear her?' Sammy greeted him. 'She seems to be in a boat. I heard her say something about being adrift. And no one could swim far in that sea.'

'Don't you come down here,' Drake panted out. 'You get back to the house. What are you doing out of bed anyway?' And he ran off down the dark path, flashing the beam of his torch ahead to guide him. 'Go home, do you hear?' he ordered again, without turning his head, when he heard Sammy following him.

Drake knew that the army notices warning of mines on the shore were genuine. He had talked to some of the sappers who had carried out the dangerous work, and even seen some of the mines being dug into the pebbles above high-water level. But it was quite clear to Drake that he had to go to Gillian's rescue, just as it was essential that Sammy's life must not be endangered.

'For the last time, go home, do you hear?'

There was no reply from Sammy, but still the footsteps thudded behind him down the zigzagging path, and Drake was helpless in the face of this sudden show of stubbornness – and sudden demonstration of speed, too, for his brother was not lagging behind.

Sammy scrambled over the gunpost, which had baulked Gillian, leapt off the other side, jumped over a wide slit trench without hesitation, darted in and out of a line of concrete anti-tank obstructions. He was still hard on Drake's heels when he sprinted across the wide Madeira Drive and was brought to a sudden halt on the far side by the high rolls of barbed-wire entanglements which stretched from end to end of the sea front.

Drake turned and shone his torch on Sammy, standing panting his heart out beside him. 'Look, will you please go home, Sammy,' Drake begged. 'This is going to be dangerous, and –'

'I think a . . . wide plank . . .' Sammy managed to get out, 'will . . . do it.'

'What do you mean?'

'If we let it fall . . . on the wire –'

Drake hesitated. 'Yes, of course.' He had to admit to himself that this was the only answer.

Gillian's cries were sounding nearer now, and Drake broke off his search with the torch to call back, 'All right, we're coming.'

It was Sammy who found two ten-foot planks in a dump of army material, and with Drake carrying one under his arm and Sammy dragging the other, they got them back across the road.

'All right, let them go now,' Drake ordered, and the planks fell together like a drawbridge on to the top of the wire. Drake, with one foot on each plank, began feeling his way cautiously up the slope, which became less steep the higher he climbed as his weight pressed down on the wire.

'You're to stay where you are, do you understand?' he called back to Sammy. 'There's a minefield on the other side and there's no point in us both being blown up.' He was steadying himself by holding strands of the wire, making his way cautiously over their makeshift bridge, and quite unaware of the fact that Sammy was close behind. 'Wonder what on earth the girl's up to,' he went on, speaking half to himself as an aid to concentration, for this was a balancing operation that required some finesse, 'drifting about the sea in the middle of the night. I had an idea she might do something mad. . . .'

Drake was at the end of the plank, which had now pressed the barbed-wire rolls almost to the ground, leaving him nothing worse than a three-foot jump to the ground on the other side. 'As soon as I can find out what's going on,' he called, speaking unnaturally loudly because he thought his brother was still on the pavement of the Madeira Drive instead of following a foot behind him like a silent shadow, 'I'll try to get her ashore and bring her back this way. . . .'

And with that, Drake jumped to the ground, unbalancing Sammy, who swayed from side to side, nearly fell into the barbed wire, and finally took a flying leap forward to land beside him.

'All right, sorry, but you wobbled,' Sammy answered Drake's angry outburst, speaking with some heat and for the first time since they had set off down the slope. 'Anyway, I can't go back now, look.'

And it was all too clear to Drake that neither of them could return the way they had come, for the planks, relieved of their weight, had sprung up again, and the ends were far out of reach.

'Well, you're to stay here, you're not to move an inch,' Drake said in exasperation. 'Do you understand?' he demanded fiercely, shining the torch beam on to Sammy's small, expressionless face.

But Sammy would not be drawn, only watching in silence as his brother turned away, leapt the narrow-gauge track of Volk's electric railway and disappeared among the upturned fishermen's boats and small wooden huts at the top of the beach.

The mines, Drake knew, had been sown thickly all along this part of the shore above high-water level; and he knew that to step on one would mean instant death. But what else could he do, with Gillian's cries of distress reaching him through the sound of the waves breaking in long white lines of spray below him?

'Hold on, I'm coming,' he yelled at the top of his voice, and began running clumsily across the pebbles towards the sea. It was no use being cautious, no use treading warily or trying to avoid the invisible death-traps; his fate was out of his hands.

Drake leapt from the edge of a high ridge of pebbles and ran on as fast as he could over the loose surface, scattered with seaweed and flotsam, and halted just beyond the line of breaking surf. The waves were higher than he had thought, driven up into dark, white-capped crests by the strong westerly wind, and curling to crash in unhurried succession on to the beach. In this sea Gillian would go under within seconds. If only he could see where she was!

To the right the pattern of fairy lights from the head of the Palace Pier shone out; and to the left, farther away and in violent contrast to their gaiety, the flash of gunfire and the waving beams of the searchlights of the battle sent a glow across the horizon.

'Where are you?' Drake called; but any reply was lost in the noise of the pounding waves and the crunching of the pebbles in their backwash. Oblivious to the water swirling over his ankles, he searched the dark sea for a sign of Gillian.

At last he caught a glimpse of a small boat on a wave crest, outlined against the blaze of battle. It hung there for only a brief second, disappearing almost at once, but it was enough to give Drake its rough position.

At once Drake undid his shoes and started to strip off his jersey. It was going to be a long, tough swim. 'All right, I'm coming,' he called again, but only because the sound of his own voice was somehow reassuring. 'Don't worry, I'll be with you,' he called into the woollen jersey as he struggled to pull it over his head. But could he ever battle his way through those great waves?

His hands were on his belt buckle when he heard Sammy just behind him. 'Give me a hand, will you?' Sammy asked, his voice strained with the effort of pushing the rowing boat over the last flat stretch of beach.

'I told you –' Drake began crossly; and gave up. It was dangerous enough to walk straight across a minefield, and only Sammy could have pushed a boat through and survived. But this was certainly no time to start an argument, and Drake again had to confess that he had been an ass not to think of doing the same thing himself. Besides, Sammy seemed to have taken command of operations. 'It'll be all right if we can keep her head into the seas,' he told Drake in an authoritative voice, remembering the way the fishermen used to launch their boats in rough weather, calling to one another and timing the moment exactly. 'You steady her bows and I'll look after the stern. Jump in and grab the oars when I give the word. You're stronger than me, you'd better row.'

They slipped the boat into the receding water of an expended wave, ran her into deeper water on the suck, turned as the next breaker raced towards them and took its impact against their bent backs.

'Keep her going,' Sammy yelled, 'don't let her bows turn.' They were up to their waists in the swirling water, and Sammy was half-blinded by the spray on his spectacles as he glanced behind him to judge the moment for their next move.

'Right,' he called, 'in you get!' He watched Drake leap over the gunwale, reach down for the oars and slip them into the rowlocks. 'Pull with your right.'

Then, as the next roller curved over like a collapsing

wall, forcing the bows up at a crazy angle, Sammy lifted himself over the stern and grabbed the rudder ropes. The bows crashed down again and they swept into the next trough, with Drake pulling against the oars with all his strength.

They had shipped a good deal of water, but they were over the worst part. 'Here comes another – hold your oars,' Sammy ordered, and steered the boat up and over safely.

Once clear of the breakers, Sammy bobbed up from the stern seat every few seconds, to try and locate Gillian, at the same time shouting, 'Where are you?' If she was adrift, the wind would be blowing her east, and he set course at an angle to the shore and to the never-ending procession of advancing waves.

They found her at last, half a mile out from the shore, the lifeboat rising and falling and spinning helplessly round and round. 'Ship oars and put your torch on her,' Sammy told Drake. 'She's fifty yards ahead. See her?'

Drake balanced himself in the rocking boat and with his torch held high, shone the beam over the water. Yes, there she was, lying slumped in the stern, one arm raised in a lethargic wave of greeting. That wasn't like Gillian. The rolling of the boat appeared to have been too much for her, Drake judged.

'Be with you in a second,' he called out encouragingly, and bent back to his oars. 'Take us alongside, and we'll ship her aboard,' he told Sammy.

But Drake received no answer from his brother, who was standing with legs wide apart, balancing himself skilfully against the roll and pitch, the rudder ropes grasped in his hands. Nor could Drake see the expression of grim concentration on his face.

The enemy fleet had been annihilated. Only a scattering of blazing hulks remained, and they would soon be at the bottom. Commander Hartford's destroyer had accounted for three of them. He had taken his little ship through the smoke-screen regardless of the appalling danger, had closed with the enemy line on a cunning zigzagging course, every gun pounding out salvo after deadly salvo. At point-blank range, with the enemy shells churning the sea into a boiling cauldron on all sides, he had given the command: 'FIRE!' – and the torpedoes, those long, grey messengers of death, had shot into the water, straight towards the towering hull of the cruiser. . . .

Twice more his ship had attacked, each time with unerring aim. And now, with the battle won, the destroyer was speeding on its errand of mercy, seeking survivors on the blood-soaked ocean. 'Lifeboat ahoy!' came the look-out's cry.

'*Full astern!*' Sammy ordered – and Drake backed the oars, and at once shipped them as the two boats came alongside.

'Oh, I do feel awful,' Gillian groaned, crawling along the bottom of the lifeboat towards Drake.

'Well, hurry up,' he answered her unsympathetically. 'I can't hold the boats together much longer.' They were turning and drifting as uncontrollably as the lifeboat and the water was breaking over the sides. 'Sammy, give her a hand.'

Helped by Sammy, Gillian managed to get one leg over the gunwale and tumbled sprawling at Drake's feet. 'Thanks,' she said weakly and more decisively, 'I don't like the sea. It makes me sick!'

'We haven't risked our necks to save you from being seasick,' Drake said with a trace of asperity. 'And anyway it's a long haul to the shore.' He pulled the boat around and dug the oars into the water. But he had pulled only a few strokes before he realized that they could not possibly hope to find in the dark the exact spot where they had launched the boat, let alone retrace their course, step by step, through the minefield. They had been amazingly fortunate to survive one passage of the beach, and he could never risk their lives by attempting another.

Perhaps they could land on one of the groynes that

149

reached out into the sea at intervals along the beach? But the shore beyond was a danger zone, too, and they would still have to face the wire entanglements. That was no good.

'Come on,' Sammy called. 'Do you want me to take over? We'll capsize if you don't keep way on.'

'No, it's all right. But we'll have to make for the pier.'

This succeeded in renewing Gillian's interest in life. 'The pier?' she exclaimed, her seasickness suddenly forgotten. 'If you knew what just happened to me, if you took any interest –'

'But we are interested,' Drake said. 'It was you who didn't seem interested, rolling about as if you'd been on a raft for a month –'

'Well, I found Kensington,' she went on triumphantly as if Drake had never spoken, squatting down on the stern seat beside Sammy. 'Only the Foulshams found me at the same time. And do you know, they're not feeding her on candy floss. I can't think why, but they seem to be looking after her fairly well. She was in the shooting gallery, with some carrots and grass, and quite a decent-sized hutch, and –'

Sammy steered the boat towards the lighted pier-head while Drake pulled steadily on the oars, waiting patiently for a break in the flow of narrative. When

Gillian paused for breath he asked, 'And how, may I ask, do you know about your rabbit?'

'Oh, I climbed up. Easy. But I can't understand why they're looking after her so well.'

'Fattening it up for the stew-pot, of course,' Drake said in an off-hand voice.

This succeeded in momentarily silencing his sister. 'Do you really think so?' she asked in horror.

'Well, we'll soon find out,' Sammy said, his mind already on the dodgem cars. 'If they don't stop us from landing.'

'Or if there's any pier left for us to land on,' Drake said, dropping the oars and looking up in the direction of the sound of the screaming aircraft which had suddenly flown in very low and fast from the Channel towards them. 'It looks as if they're going to attack it.'

But Drake was wrong. There seemed to be two planes. One of them appeared to be on fire, and the wings of the second one were sparkling with the flashes of its guns. But everything that followed occurred at such bewildering speed that it was impossible to piece together their sequence. The leading aircraft shot barely a hundred feet above their boat, so low that they could make out its dark silhouette against the lighter sky, the sound of its engine rising to a crescendo. Then it disappeared from sight, reappearing as a ball of flame high over the town, the engine note suddenly extinguished by a muffled explosion.

The second circled low over the pier ahead of them, its engine racing and cutting out in turn, its course marked by bright blue exhaust flashes. Then its engine cut for the last time, and almost simultaneously with the impact of its crash into the sea, a white plume of water was thrown up.

Without a word Drake grabbed for the oars and began rowing again, digging the blades deep into the water with frenzied speed. 'Aim straight for the head of the pier,' he called out to Sammy. 'There's a coil of rope somewhere in the bottom of the boat, Gillian. Have it ready in case we need it.'

It was hard going into the teeth of the wind and Drake felt little hope that they would get there in time to be of any use. Modern metal aircraft sank quickly, he had heard, but the pilot appeared to have ditched as close to the pier as he could in the hope of being able to climb on to it.

Slowly, agonizingly slowly, the lights of the pier came closer. From the stern, Sammy and Gillian could hear the sound of shouting and see scurrying figures on the promenade above. 'Throw over a lifebelt,' he heard a voice call, and another answered, 'It's too far. Can you see it?'

'Keep a sharp look-out,' Drake ordered. He glanced over his shoulder at the pillars and girders of the pier's structure that seemed to tower above them. 'We must be near the spot now.'

'There it is,' Sammy suddenly called out, pointing over to their right and nearly toppling into the sea in his excitement. 'Give me the torch.'

The white beam skimmed the wave-tops, flickered left and right, hesitated – caught the wing-tip projecting at a sharp angle out of the water. 'Here, hold it like that, don't lose it,' Sammy told Gillian, carefully handing her the torch. 'Pull away, I'll steer you there,' he said to Drake.

A few dozen more strong pulls brought them alongside the foundering wreckage; consisting of a bent and twisted tail-section, the fuselage as far forward as the cockpit, the single surviving wing that was peppered with bullet holes.

'Can you see him? Give me the torch,' Drake demanded. 'The hood's open.' At first the cockpit appeared to be empty, and the torch beam revealed only the instrument panel, the gun-sight above it, and the control stick. But as their boat drifted close alongside and Sammy reached out to grab hold of the top of the rudder, Drake saw the legs that were half in and half out of the cockpit, the body slumped over the far side of the fuselage. And a wave of sick horror flooded his mind.

He must be dead, Drake told himself. He ought to land Sammy and Gillian on the pier and come back for the corpse . . . he could tackle it by himself . . . but he mustn't let them see.

'Is he dead, do you think?' Sammy said calmly, as if asking the time of the day.

'I don't know. I think so. He's not moving. I'll drop you on the landing stage first, I think.'

'Don't be an ass,' Gillian told him crossly. 'You can't lift him out by yourself. Anyway, it's sinking. Come on for goodness' sake. I'm going to see.' And before Drake could prevent her, she made a jump for the plane's fuselage, landed safely on all fours, and began to balance walk along its narrow, rocking back.

They saw her ease herself round the cockpit canopy, which had been slid back as far as it would go, and drop down into the seat beside the dangling legs of the pilot.

'He doesn't look too bad,' she said, leaning over the side and shining the torch on to his face. 'Just a bit wet, like me. Come and give me a hand, one of you, he's heavy.'

They did not dare to lash the boat to the wreckage in case it sank, and this meant that only two of them could struggle to lift the limp body of the pilot, while Sammy held the rocking, swaying boat loosely against the side of the fuselage.

154

'Goodness, what a weight!' Gillian exclaimed, heaving with all her might at the fur collar of the pilot's flying jacket. She was standing awkwardly on the tilted wing, which was sinking deeper and deeper as the cockpit filled, up to her waist in water, while Drake leaned down from astride the perspex canopy to drag at the limp arms.

After what seemed like an interminable length of time, they managed to drag him into a sitting position, half in and half out of the cockpit, so that Drake could lean over and slip his hand under the flying jacket. But he did not need to feel the beating heart to know that the man was alive; his warm breath, carrying the scent of tobacco, played gently against Drake's cheek, causing him to wonder for one fleeting – and whimsical – moment where the pilot had smoked that last cigarette.

'It's all right, he is alive,' Drake told them. 'Can you bring the boat closer?' he asked Sammy. 'This part'll be difficult, and we're going under any second.'

The plane lurched another twenty degrees, completely submerging the cockpit and leaving only the head and shoulders of the pilot out of the water. 'Get the rope under his armpits, quick,' Drake said. 'We might be able to drag him to the pier then.' If only the wreckage would cease rocking, if only the pilot's limbs weren't so heavy!

'Twice round – O.K.? Don't worry about knotting it. Now, both together – heave!' But it was quite hopeless. They just did not have the strength to raise by as much as an inch the heavy pilot in his waterlogged flying clothes.

None of the Hartfords thought the moment would come when they would welcome the sound of Arthur Foulsham's voice. But at the cry of, 'Tally ho! – we're coming!' Drake and Gillian turned in relief from their hopelessly unequal struggle, and Sammy actually waved and let out a cheer when he saw the packed boat-load of children approaching from the landing stage.

As usual, the Foulshams were doing things in style. There was a lamp at the masthead of the big boat, and two more at the stem and stern, and the four of them who were not at the oars were crowded in the bows chanting,

> 'Here come the Foulshams
> Full of good deeds,
> First aid or charity,
> Beneficent philanthropy,
> Call in the Foulshams for all your needs.'

'Well, hurry up then,' Gillian called to them. 'We're going under.'

The singing died before the boat halted, and at once five of the largest Foulshams, followed by two more, plunged overboard with squeals of joy and struck out through the rough seas for the wreckage.

Eleanor was the first to scramble aboard. They saw her grab a spar of the shattered tail-plane and lift herself out of the sea, her red hair falling in sodden rats' tails across her face. She turned and lowered a hand to haul up Jeremy. 'Many hands make light work,' she sang out – and was promptly unbalanced by the weight on her arm and tumbled back into the sea.

'Serves you right for spouting potty platitudes,' Arthur laughed, with his mouth half full of water, and helped her up on to the wreckage again. All round the plane the sea was like the shallow end of Black Rock swimming pool at the height of the holiday season, with all but one of the Foulshams, who remained in charge of the boat, splashing and threshing about, struggling to get on to the fuselage.

'Hey, you'll sink us!' Gillian called out. They seemed to be treating the rescue operation as a game and to have forgotten that the pilot's life was at stake.

But strength of numbers counted in the end, and in their wild, disorganized way, pulling and heaving at the unconscious form amid a cacophony of shouted commands and counter-commands, shrieks and yells, they succeeded in lifting the pilot from the submerged cockpit and rolling him over the gunwale into the lifeboat.

From his precarious foothold half-way up the tilted wing, Arthur Foulsham looked down with satisfaction at the prostrate form spread out on the bottom of the boat. 'A job worth doing is worth doing well, is what I always say,' he said lightly. 'There's another one for the storehouse of potty platitudes, Eleanor. I think we'd better get the old boy ashore, don't you?' he asked, turning to Drake, who was still up to his waist in the cockpit. 'The hospital facilities are not of the most modern on the pier, and he looks rather in need of a warm bed.'

'Will you show us where you land on the beach then?' Drake answered, unconscious of the fact that for the first time he was carrying on a normal conversation with a Foulsham. 'I suppose you've got a marked passage through the minefield, too.'

'I don't know about any minefield,' Arthur said. 'But we had to spend hours cutting a hole through a lot of silly wire to get on to the beach. It was the only way of getting on to the pier. We'll lead the way, and you follow with our gallant wounded aeronaut in the lifeboat, O.K.?'

The wing tipped at a more acute angle, causing Arthur to lose his hold and come sliding down into the water.

'She's going down!' Randolph called from the rudder. 'Abandon ship – each man for himself.'

As the fuselage slipped deeper and deeper into the waves, Drake and Gillian clambered back into their boat, while the Foulshams slipped into the water one after the other and began swimming towards their boat, their progress accompanied by much shouting, and delayed by a good deal of splashing and ducking.

Once they were all safely aboard (and Drake noticed that a larger Foulsham would frequently help up a smaller one after a merciless ducking), Arthur made his way to the bows, and, standing beside the lantern with one foot on the prow like a Viking captain, pointed an arm at the last piece of wreckage sticking out of the sea. 'Please raise your hats, ladies and gentlemen,' he ordered in a solemn voice. 'Pray silence in honour of this heroic machine, so soon to be drawn down to her eternal grave. She fought bravely,' he added with a heavy sob, 'she was a good plane!'

Suddenly the shattered tail section lifted vertically up out of the waves as if responding to the mock salute, remained poised for several seconds, and then plunged out of sight.

'Farewell, noble scourge of the skies,' Arthur called, waving an arm; and Sammy, Gillian, and Drake all found themselves joining in the cheer before oars were slipped into rowlocks again, and the two boats began making their way through the waves towards the head of the pier.

Gillian sat in the bottom of the boat, cradling the pilot's head in her lap. She had slipped off his helmet and with the torch in one hand had tried to dry his face with a sodden handkerchief. 'He's got a horrible cut in his forehead,' she said, bending closer over the pilot. 'Look, Drake. And I think he's coming round,' she added more excitedly.

'Yes, his eyes are opening.'

'Probably just concussion,' Drake answered, pulling back on the oars. It was hard going trying to keep up with the Foulshams' boat ahead of them. 'I expect he caught his head on the gun-sight when he hit the sea.'

Even viewed from upside down by the fading light of the torch, Gillian decided it looked a pleasant face, clean-shaven, very fair and very young. 'How do you feel?' she asked the man softly, twisting her head round so that he could see her from the right way up.

The pale lips formed into a smile. 'My – head – hurts,' he said slowly. 'Otherwise all right. A bit cold. Did – was it you – who pulled me out?'

'Well, no. A lot of us did, really. You just lie quietly. We'll soon have you in a nice warm bed.'

They were rounding the head of the pier, passing the

landing stage where the pleasure steamers used to tie up, and where the Foulshams must have kept their boat. Gillian looked up at the lighted pier above them – and suddenly remembered.

'Drake,' she said. 'Now's our chance. We can't leave Kensington up there all alone.'

'We're not going to stop for that rabbit of yours,' he answered shortly. 'Wretched thing's caused us enough trouble, and –'

'Oh, please. Please – I'll jump overboard if you don't,' she threatened. 'It won't take a minute. You wouldn't mind if we stopped so I can get back my rabbit?' she asked the pilot in a pleading voice. 'You see – oh, it's rather a long story.'

The man raised his head painfully from Gillian's lap and addressed himself to Drake. 'Of course she must have her rabbit,' he said, managing to give a wan smile. 'I am sure it – it is very important – and I'm all right.'

Drake held the oars above the water and looked over his shoulder at the receding lights of the Foulshams' boat, which was already heading for the beach on the west side of the pier. 'Oh, all right then. But for goodness' sake hurry. . . .'

'Here they come at last,' they heard Arthur call to the other Foulshams who were standing impatiently beside

161

the boat which they had drawn up on to the beach. 'Been for a day trip to France?' he shouted out over the breaking rollers.

The boat was lifted up on to the crest of a wave and carried forward at an accelerating speed. 'Ship your oars,' Sammy cried from the stern, pulling the rudder ropes left and right in turn to keep them on a straight course.

The wave began curling under them, carrying them forward faster and faster on its swirling foam-capped peak. Then the stem touched the pebbles, and the hull rattled on the shore as they were swept high up the beach and left stranded by the receding water, surrounded by chattering Foulshams.

'Oh, so that's what you've been up to!' Eleanor greeted Gillian, looking down at the rabbit in her arms. She was laughing without rancour. 'I might have guessed. How are you, dear Van Gogh?' she cooed at the animal in Gillian's arms and stroked its head. 'Hope you weren't as seasick coming ashore as you were going out.'

'Soused in sentiment – hopeless, aren't they?' Arthur confided in Drake as he tucked his arms under the pilot's shoulders. 'Come on, gasbags. Lend a hand. Florence Nightingale would turn in her grave if she could see you.'

Between them they lifted the man out of the lifeboat and placed him gently on the pebbles. 'I'm all right, really – just a bit – a bit dizzy,' he told them, trying to sit up. 'It's my head, you know.'

By the light of the lantern held over him by Jeremy his face looked deathly pale and his lips had turned bright blue. 'He's shivering, poor chap,' the nine-year-old Sybil said in an anxious voice, with one hand on his wrist to feel his pulse. Unlike Eleanor, she had nursing ambitions.

Drake bent over the pilot's head and examined the long wound carefully. 'I think I'd better do something about this before we move him,' he said. The man seemed weaker now than when he had first regained consciousness, and his eyes were half-closed. He had read in a copy of his father's *British Medical Journal* that pilots sometimes carried first-aid kits in their flying clothing, and Drake began feeling inside the fur-lined jacket.

'In – the – leg,' he heard the man whisper softly, and Drake slipped a hand into a deep thigh pocket. Holding the torch between his teeth, he drew out the square, watertight package and began stripping off the cover.

Most of the Foulshams were scouring the beach in search of timber from which to make a stretcher, and neither Sammy nor Gillian noticed Drake hesitate before hurriedly ripping off the cover of the first-aid packet and stuffing it away in his trouser pocket.

Only Drake saw the printed instructions under the familiar Red Cross on the outside.

'*Achtung!*' they began, '*Zum Notgebrauch!*'

8

Van Gogh Comes Home

AND yet he seems quite an ordinary chap, Drake was thinking as he cleaned the deep wound with some antiseptic from a little tube. He had been grateful to them for rescuing him, and for someone who had faced what must have appeared certain death he had behaved bravely.

Drake raised the limp head, helped by the assiduous Sybil, and unrolled the bandage round and round. The wound badly needed stitching but there was nothing he could do about that.

It was difficult to associate this polite young man with one of the desperate warriors he had imagined fighting their way on to British soil on the morning of the invasion. This pilot did not look as though he would shoot a mouse with the big Luger automatic protruding from the holster at his waist. . . . He had spoken perfect

English, too. He must have spent some time in England before the war, perhaps as an exchange student at a British university.

Drake stared closely at the pale-skinned face with the rather prominent cheekbones, and at the same moment the pilot opened his eyes, blinking in the light of the torch. 'Thank you,' he said again very softly. 'I am more comfortable now.'

'All right, Drake, got something. We can carry him on these.' It was Arthur, lugging two long bits of timber and leading a crowd of his brothers and sisters back across the beach. At all events Drake must not let the Foulshams know that they had a prisoner-of-war on their hands. They were so wild there was no telling what they might do to him. . . .

When they had succeeded in rolling the half-conscious pilot on to the lengths of driftwood, Sammy and six of the Foulshams raised him carefully from the ground and with Arthur in front and Drake walking alongside the makeshift stretcher, they made their way up the beach towards the lower promenade.

Behind the party, Eleanor and Gillian were discussing, without heat, the mystery of the identity of the white rabbit, which still lay in apparent contentment in Gillian's arms.

'But honestly, I bought her in the market – for three-

and-six, and two of Rosemary's last babies,' Gillian was saying.

'Well then, it must be just an odd coincidence that Van Gogh disappeared that very morning.' There was a trace of suspicion in Eleanor's voice, which disappeared when she suddenly turned excitedly and said, 'I know, I expect the market man *stole* him.'

Gillian considered this for a moment. Then she said, 'No, that's not the answer. He'd had her for at least a week before I bought her. I was just waiting for enough pocket money.'

They were still trying to solve the problem as Arthur pulled aside a section of the barbed-wire barrier on the promenade, revealing their secret way down to the shore. It would have required a close examination to discover where they had painstakingly severed the strands.

'Welcome to Brighton,' Arthur said with a bow as the party made its way through the gap towards the slope leading to the sea front. 'Sunny, salubrious Brighton, Queen of Watering Places – and as dead as dear old Prinnie himself. Where are you going to take your patient?' he asked Drake.

Jeremy Foulsham let out a groan. 'Anywhere – but not much farther than this,' he begged. 'He weighs a ton.'

'I think we'd better go to our house,' Drake said after

a moment's thought. 'We've got a fire going so that we can boil some water to wash his wound.'

'I'm going on strike then,' Randolph said firmly. 'That's too far.'

Drake looked up and down the sea front, and his eye was caught by the twin headlamp beams of the armoured car still shining purposelessly on to the pier entrance. 'There you are!' he said in triumph. 'Our besieging vehicle. We can stretch him out on the seats, and with all of us pushing we can get it up on to the Marine Parade.'

Arthur held the boat lantern he had been carrying above Drake's head. 'By golly!' he exclaimed in awe, studying his face in close-up, 'these horrid Hartfords aren't so totally lacking in brain-power as we'd thought. They have almost, I have to confess, shown themselves worthy to be Foulshams tonight.' And his brothers and sisters roared agreement.

An hour or two earlier they might all have missed the collapsed parachute. But a touch of dawn was showing over the cliffs towards Rottingdean when they breasted the rise of the Marine Parade (all eleven of them heaving at the armoured car), and in that first faint light they could not miss the white spread of silk lying across the roof of the Aquarium below.

In fact, so many Foulshams impulsively left the armoured car to run to the railings that Drake only just managed to leap into the driving seat and haul on the brake in time to prevent it from running backwards down the hill again.

'Look, here's a body beside it,' Eleanor exclaimed with relish. 'What a night we're having. Come on, perhaps this one *is* dead.'

Arthur led the easy climb down and bent over the still form lying spread-eagled on the tarred roof. 'He's alive all right,' he said quietly, 'though not in the best of health I'd say. Stand back, everybody. You'll suffocate the poor chap. You're the expert, you take a look, Drake.'

Drake bent down and lifted back the gauntlet glove to feel for the man's pulse. It was beating, rather faintly but regularly. 'Yes, he's all right. But his leg looks bad, so lift him very gently.'

He stood beside Arthur, watching anxiously as half a dozen Foulshams turned the pilot on to his back and lifted him into a sitting position. The familiar R.A.F. wings were clearly visible on the left breast of his uniform.

'What a laugh it'd be,' Arthur said to Drake, 'if these two both came round in the armoured car and started going hammer and tongs at one another again.'

'What do you mean?' Drake asked.

'Well, that's what they ought to do by rights, poor chumps,' Arthur replied. 'Better relieve them of their weapons, I suppose.'

'Do you mean you knew the first pilot was a German, then?' Drake asked in amazement.

Arthur raised one of the unconscious man's legs which was trailing on the ground as he was carried across the roof. 'Of course. Here, take this leg, Vincent, and don't let it drop,' he told his brother. 'Didn't you see the swastika on the plane's tail? This chap must have baled out of the plane that blew up over the town. What a silly business it is! Neither of them's won, and they've both lost.' He gave a short laugh. 'Might just as well not have started scrapping at all.'

Drake, too stunned to reply, followed Arthur back to the armoured car in silence. It was quite curious enough to find himself drawn by a sudden crisis into this new relationship with Arthur and the rest of the Foulshams. But what he was discovering about the family in their new intimacy was even more curious. Perhaps they were coarse and brash and ill-mannered; but, with their *joie de vivre* and brilliant ideas, these Foulshams did seem to get the most out of life . . . and Arthur himself wasn't, after all, just the brutish windbag Drake had always imagined him to be.

'Whoa, hold it, lads and lassies,' Arthur told those carrying the R.A.F. pilot as they succeeded at last in getting him over the railings. 'Let's get the door open for you. Any more for the blood-wagon?' he called out. 'Hurry, hurry, we're nearly full up.'

Gillian, who was standing behind him, tried to suppress a giggle. So long as you weren't at the receiving end of his jibes and aggressive humour, she was thinking, you had to admit he was rather fun. 'Here, *ouvrez la porte*, thou bunny fancier,' he ordered Gillian; and, passing Kensington to Eleanor with a brief 'Hold her a second, will you,' she did as she was told.

'Well, I don't know about everyone else, but I've had about enough of lugging bodies about the place for one night,' Jeremy Foulsham said when they had at last succeeded in getting the R.A.F. pilot tucked into Mr Hartford's bed.

It had been a long, tiring business first to haul the armoured car back along the Marine Parade, and then to lift the two men out and carry them up the flight of stairs and into the front bedroom of Adelaide House. But now, standing in the dawn half-light in a semicircle about the twin beds, the eight Foulshams and Sammy, Drake, and Gillian surveyed their patients with some satisfaction.

'Mother would have a fit if she could see this,' Drake said, and Gillian laughed at the idea of Mrs Hartford, who was particularly fastidious, contemplating a fully dressed German fighter pilot with a dirty bandage round his forehead in her dainty bed, with its Irish linen sheets and fine old lace counterpane.

The German had fully recovered consciousness before they arrived home, and had felt so much better that he had tried to walk upstairs, although the solicitous Foulshams had insisted on carrying him. He was sitting up now, the R.A.F. pilot still unconscious in the bed alongside, chatting to them with what seemed to be a forced cheerfulness.

'Your clothes are still sopping wet. Why won't you put on these pyjamas?' Drake asked him again. 'My father wouldn't mind.' They had tried several times to persuade him to take off his flying jacket, but he had stubbornly refused.

'No, I like my furry jacket,' he said with a laugh. 'It keeps me snug.'

'How's the battle going?' Arthur asked.

'The battle?' the pilot asked. He gave a quick nervous laugh. 'Oh, I think we'll drive them back into the sea all right.'

Arthur looked perplexed. 'What on earth do you mean? You've got it round the wrong way. I thought we were trying to drive you back into the sea,' he said.

A look of fear came into the German's face. His bright blue eyes darted defensively round the circle of faces. 'Well . . .' he began awkwardly.

Suddenly Arthur burst out laughing. 'Oh, I see!' he exclaimed. 'You still think we think you're an English pilot just because you talk English. What a joke!' He turned to the others. 'So that's why he wouldn't take off his flying jacket. He thought we'd see his uniform.' He sat down on the edge of the pilot's bed. 'Cheer up,' he told him. 'We don't care a rap whether you're German or Tibetan. I suppose you were told we ate captured German pilots to eke out our rations. And talking of rations,' Arthur said with sudden zeal, 'I must eat. We must all eat. Fritz here must eat. Let's have a gargantuan feast, eh Drake? What've you got?'

Arthur Foulsham leapt up from the bed and strode across the deep carpet to the door. 'Lead us to your provisions, horrid Hartfords. We'll bring you up something, Fritz, don't worry. And for goodness' sake put those pyjamas on now before you catch your death of cold.'

Drake was the last to leave the room, and before shutting the door behind him he gave the German a friendly wave. There was still an expression of incredulity

. . . and then to lift the two men out

on his pale face, as if he only half believed that the succession of events during the night, which had been mostly experienced in a state of semi-consciousness, was nothing but a weird dream. 'You are very kind,' he said weakly, and allowed his head to fall back on to the piled-up pillows.

The preparations for breakfast were carried out in the characteristic Foulsham manner, although, rather to their surprise, neither Sammy, Gillian, nor Drake minded the unprecedented sound that filled the kitchen and the downstairs rooms of the house. The sight of Foulshams burrowing about in the larders and cupboards, rushing up and down the basement stairs, climbing over the drawing-room furniture, struck the Hartfords as odd rather than offensive – and stimulating, too, Drake decided. Adelaide House seemed now a good deal less forlorn than it had when they were occupying it alone.

Somehow, in their wild, disorganized way, the Foulshams, assisted by directions from Drake and Gillian, succeeded in getting a large and hot meal in a surprisingly short time. The drawing-room fire was built up to a blaze, on which four large saucepans full of tinned soup were heated. A dozen more tins of meat and fruit were spread on the Sheraton coffee table (protected, at Drake's insistence, by newspapers). And as the sun rose above the houses on the other side of Lewes Crescent, they all began the strenuous business of eating.

Eleanor, perched on the back of an armchair with a plate on her knees, glanced curiously about the room. 'This is what I call stylish living,' she said, the note of appreciation in her voice muffled by corned beef and baked beans. 'Even got carpets on the floor – see that, Arthur?'

'And look at all the chintz and the silver ash-trays and what-nots.' Arthur, who was sitting by the window, rubbed the curtains between his fingers. 'Real velvet, too. Though I don't know what George would think of those pictures.'

George Foulsham (always referred to by his Christian name) would not have approved, Gillian decided. Victorian water-colour landscapes wouldn't be his cup of tea at all.

'You must come over and see our old junk hole some time,' Arthur suggested to Drake. 'What George calls basic Bohemian living – no ruling-class frills for our George. A bit of lino in the studio to keep the draught out, and that's about all. Oh, but the pier – now that was real luxury! Snug as bugs in a rug in that old theatre, we were. We converted one of the dressing-rooms into a kitchen and ate on the stage. And every form of entertainment on the doorstep. We must take you out there when we've got rid of our wounded.'

Drake got up from the floor with his empty plate. 'Talking of our wounded, I'd better go and see about them,' he said. 'Fetch a tray, will you, Gillian? Some soup won't do him any harm. And bring two bowls in case the other one's better.' He turned to Arthur. 'What on earth are we going to do with them, do you suppose?' he asked him. 'We can't keep them here for ever, and they really ought to have proper medical attention. I only know a bit of first aid and what I've picked up from my father.'

Arthur finished licking his finger before answering. 'It'll all come out in the wash,' he said lightly. 'All's for the best in the best of all possible worlds. There you are – two more potty platitudes for your collection, Eleanor,' he added grinning at his sister.

Conversation had become general again when Drake and Gillian left the room with the tray; which meant, with the Foulshams, that not less than four were talking at once.

The R.A.F. pilot's eyes were open when they entered the bedroom. 'He says he's feeling all right,' Fritz told them with obvious pleasure, almost as if he had been responsible for the cure. 'It's just that his leg hurts, isn't that right, Freddy?'

'Freddy? Is that your name?' Gillian asked, going over and sitting on his bed. He had a narrow, dark face, with a wide handlebar moustache on his upper lip – an alert, intelligent face, dulled now by pain. 'Freddy and Fritz, isn't that nice?'

Drake pulled back his bedclothes. 'I've done what I can,' he told Freddy. 'I've cleaned it up, but I'm afraid you've got a compound fracture of the tibia. And the bone's broken through the flesh too.'

Freddy tried to look down at his wounded leg, but the effort required was too great. 'Thanks very much, anyway, lad,' he said to Drake. 'Do you think you'd better telephone the hospital?'

Drake laughed. 'That's no good, I'm afraid. There are plenty of hospitals, but you'd find life rather lonely. We're the only people in Brighton, you see.'

'You – you the only –?'

'Yes, the town was evacuated when the invasion began, but we missed the last train. And lucky for you we did.'

'But there were a lot of lights on the pier,' Freddy said, still only half believing Drake. 'I couldn't understand it.'

'Yes, I saw them, too,' Fritz put in. 'That's why I landed in the sea there – after Freddy here put a nice long burst in my engine.'

Freddy turned his head on the pillow towards the

German and began speaking with the eagerness of a football player discussing a keen match with his opponent. 'So I did catch you with that last burst, did I? I thought I'd missed. The trouble was, you got on to my tail after I rolled off the top, and I just couldn't out-turn you. I still don't know how I threw you off, but anyway it was too late by then. I knew I was a goner.'

Fritz was leaning towards Freddy on one elbow. 'It was that sudden reverse you did when we were climbing,' he said. 'Look, we were like this –' and he began to simulate the movements of the planes with his hands until Gillian interrupted.

'You can play your games afterwards,' she told them firmly. 'But for goodness' sake have this soup while it's hot. You've both had a nasty shock, and if you don't mind my saying so, I think it's a pretty dotty business rushing round in the dark like that popping away at one another with guns. You might have been much worse hurt.'

Even by Foulsham standards, the drawing-room was in a state of uproar when Drake and Gillian came downstairs. 'But it can't be, I tell you,' Sammy was shouting indignantly. 'She couldn't possibly have got out. The back door's always kept shut, and so is the front one.'

Gillian ran into the room followed by Drake. They were all at the windows, jostling to get a clear view of the Lewes Crescent gardens.

'Well, there's the evidence before your very eyes,' Eleanor called above half a dozen piping voices. 'He knew where his home was all right. Van Gogh obviously decided he didn't like your garden and went back under his own steam. He's always been full of initiative has our Van Gogh.' She turned from the window and pushed her way through the crowd, making for the door.

'What's the matter? What about Van Gogh?' Gillian asked her as she ran past.

'Proof positive,' Eleanor told her triumphantly. 'We left Van Gogh in your back garden, and there he is nibbling the grass right in front of our house. He couldn't get in because the door's locked, but he's obviously been trying, bless his heart.' And she dashed out of the room, through the hall and out into the road.

When Eleanor came back a few minutes later with a rabbit in her arms, they were all standing on the front steps to greet her, Drake, Sammy, and Gillian silent with apprehension, the Foulshams twittering triumphantly among themselves.

'You know your rightful owner, don't you my pet?' they all heard Eleanor murmuring to the rabbit as she paused on the pavement outside the house, and then looked up at Gillian with a sympathetic smile. 'Sorry,' she said. 'But this does rather prove it, doesn't it?'

'I suppose it does,' Gillian said slowly.

Drake stepped forward from the back of the crowd and made his way down the steps towards Eleanor. 'Look, I don't know much about rabbits, in fact I always make Gillian cross by calling them "it". But I do know a bit of biology, and if Van Gogh's a he, and Kensington's a she, then surely there's only one way of settling this once and for all.'

This was met by a chorus of approval, and he was about to take the rabbit from Eleanor's arms when there was a scream from the hall of Adelaide House.

Everyone turned in alarm to see little Simon Foulsham standing at the bottom of the stairs pointing down at something at his feet. 'I opened the back door,' he called out in a high-pitched voice that was almost a squeak, 'and it just hopped in. There are *two* white rabbits – Van Gogh was lost!'

Gillian barged her way through the packed Foulshams, knocking the smaller ones flying; and tore into the hall. 'Kensington, my darling Kensington,' she cried out. 'I *knew* it was you all the time.'

9

Rob Roy

SLOWLY the shaft of sunshine stealing between the drawn curtains crept across Sammy's jersey up to his chin, over his mouth and cheeks. When it reached his eyes he woke up, blinking in the sudden dazzling rays, and turned away his face. The clock on the drawing-room mantelpiece showed five past three: an odd time and an odd place to be sleeping; but then none of them had been to bed and it had been a hectic night.

Scattered about the room in attitudes of abandon on the chairs and sofa and curled up on the floor, lay Gillian and Drake and all the Foulshams, the dishes and pans from their morning feast around them. They were all asleep, some with heads doubled awkwardly forward, some with mouths wide open; and the sound of their breathing was like the faint gusts of a breeze stirring a field of corn.

Sammy knew he would not go to sleep again. He felt wide awake after his vivid dream and ready to begin the day over again. As he sat up on the window seat, his knees tucked against his chest, he remembered that they had been discussing a problem after their feast. Then one after another the Foulshams had collapsed into an exhausted sleep, and as each lost consciousness the excited chatter had slowly died until they were all silent.

The problem under discussion, Sammy now recalled, was that of the wounded pilots upstairs. Drake had said again, and they had all agreed, that they would have to move them to a place where they could have proper medical aid. But how was this to be done, even if they had possessed some means of transport? The town was cut off from the outside world, the line of battle by now in all probability extended right across the county, barring them from London.

Jeremy Foulsham, who was regarded as something of a mechanical genius and had been responsible for starting the electric generator on the pier as well as getting the dodgems and ghost train going, had suggested that he should attempt to repair the armoured car's engine. The idea of racing up the London road through the field of battle on their mission of mercy, with guns firing, was naturally received with enthusiasm by the Foulshams.

But Drake had doubted that a boy of twelve could succeed where the army mechanics had failed.

They were in this state of indecision when, one by one, they had surrendered to their fatigue.

Sammy's dream had been a curious one, and for once it had not been a dream of being at sea or of racing into battle in a destroyer. This dream had harked back to an old enthusiasm of his; and it seemed to Sammy that it might contain the germ of an idea – an idea that could solve their dilemma.

'It might – it just might,' he said to himself as he stared across the dim-lighted drawing-room. 'Worth trying, anyway, before they wake up. Once the Foulshams are up and around it'll be impossible to do anything without being followed and questioned.'

Silently Sammy tiptoed across the deep carpet, stepping carefully between the arms and legs that lay all over the floor, and let himself out of the front door.

It was a long time since he had bicycled north through the back of Kemp Town towards the old station and the railway cuttings and tunnels that sliced their way through the mean little streets behind Queen's Park and the slopes of Race Hill. In the old days, when the railway was the great enthusiasm in his life and before he had discovered the delights of warships, he spent all his free time roaming about the sidings of Kemp Town station and the coal depot above Lewes Road, or peering down from forbidden ground above the tunnel mouths and the deep cuttings collecting engine numbers.

Sammy free-wheeled into the station yard and propped his bicycle against the wall of the old booking-office. There was nothing unusual in the deserted state of the sidings, he knew, for the Kemp Town branch had long ago been disused as a passenger station, and often when he used to visit it before the war there would be only a few trucks on the lines, one or two men desultorily unloading or loading them, with the single shunting locomotive shuttling about. It was an old 2-2-2 named Rob Roy, which Sammy used to see so often that he came to regard it with special affection. On one wonderful day, he remembered, he had been allowed a brief run on the footplate with the driver and fireman.

But Kemp Town was also something of a junk yard, and you never knew what old railway relics you might find parked on the rusty rails.

Nothing appeared to have changed since Sammy had last visited the place more than a year before. There were half a dozen trucks, still loaded with coal, standing in one of the sidings; beyond them a disused breakdown wagon. And the old Victorian third-class coach with horsehair seats full of mice nests and with oil-lamp brackets on the compartment ceilings, which he used to play in, was still there.

But what had happened to Rob Roy? Pressed into service, no doubt, to draw the train-loads of evacuees out of Brighton. Sammy ran across the lines to the crumbling wooden shed where it used to be kept, and peered through one of the broken windows. And there it was, looking dirty and neglected, as if it had not been used for months, the Gothic-lettered name over the driving-wheel shield and the tall smokestack proving its identity.

Perhaps his dream was closer to reality than he had imagined; perhaps, after all, there was something in the plan it had set off. Its success would depend on Jeremy Foulsham.

Sammy returned to Adelaide House to find a conference, accompanied by high tea, in full swing in what had become known as the hospital ward upstairs. After a further examination of the R.A.F. pilot's broken leg, Drake had told Arthur Foulsham that the question of medical attention had become one of the utmost urgency as there was a risk of gangrene setting in. Arthur had proved first that he was capable of treating serious matters seriously, which sometimes appeared hard to believe, and secondly that when necessary, his authority among his brothers and sisters was beyond question.

The Foulshams had been summoned upstairs with their plates of tea and ordered to be silent while he and Drake discussed their future plans with Fritz and Freddy. To the delight of the German, however, who was a great rabbit fancier, Kensington, Rosemary, and Van Gogh were allowed to be present, and hopped from plate to plate nibbling great quantities of unsuitable food.

Neither of the pilots was able to think of any solution to the problem, and Drake was saying, 'Perhaps I could go out on my bicycle and try to establish contact with a medical unit,' when Sammy strolled into the room, his face tense with the strain of attemping to conceal his excitement.

'And where do you think *you've* been?' Drake asked him severely.

'Exploring. I had a prophetic dream,' Sammy told them all, pleased that the announcement, which he had been carefully considering all the way home, sounded impressive. 'Do you know anything about steam locomotives?' he asked Jeremy.

'A bit. Why?' His clever little freckled face, which rarely revealed perplexity over mechanical problems, was set in a frown.

'Well, not far from here,' Sammy went on, frankly breathless now, 'there's a 2-2-2 shunting locomotive called Rob Roy, that used to work about a year ago. And there's an old coach, which has still get its wheels all right and should go. And I thought if we painted it white and put a Red Cross on the side, well I thought we could all take the injured to London. You see –'

The Foulshams had broken into a chorus of twittering, and Fritz and Freddy were smiling weakly from their pillows. 'Hold on a minute,' Drake said. 'Just what are you suggesting?'

'You remember what that corporal said at the station?' Sammy continued. 'You know, when he stopped us at the barrier? He said a Red Cross train's always safe. Then if Jeremy can get some steam up on Rob Roy . . .'

At this point Arthur interceded. He placed his half-eaten bowl of tinned pineapple on the floor and walked solemnly across to Sammy, placed a hand on his shoulder, and said in tones of mock reverence, 'It can no longer be denied that in the solid rock of horrid Hartford respectability there are veins of genius – pure genius. This is not the first evidence we have had, and we shall soon have to seriously consider inviting them into that sacred circle of brilliant geniuses, the fruity Foulshams. Initiation rites will commence at the rising of the moon in its fourth quarter on the Palace Pier dodgem track. . . .

What do you think?' he asked, suddenly turning and speaking more seriously to the pilots. 'Your life may depend on this, Freddy.'

Freddy turned his pale drawn face towards the other bed. 'Well, Fritzy boy,' he asked, 'what about it? Do we entrust our lives to this gang of madcaps?'

'They haven't done badly so far,' the German replied, smiling up at Arthur and Drake.

This was the signal for a great Foulsham outburst of cheers, and at once the frieze of tense faces surrounding the beds broke up into a mêlée of waving arms and legs and rolling, leaping figures. 'Bags drive – I'm going to be the driver,' a high-pitched voice cried out. 'Bags be guard – bags blow the whistle and wave the flag,' another Foulsham shouted. The uproar rose to a crescendo, until it seemed as if the windows must blow out. . . .

'Silence! Silence, d'you hear!' When it came to sheer volume, Arthur could outdo all his brothers and sisters combined. Slowly the sound died to a mere muttering, and one by one they turned to face the husky figure standing with legs astride on Mrs Hartford's dressing-table.

'Let us face our responsibilities,' Arthur went on, when he was satisfied that he had everyone's attention and speaking in the stirring sing-song tones of Britain's Prime Minister, Winston Churchill. 'Let us face our responsibilities with courage and stout hearts – and less ghastly noise. Sammy, will you take Jeremy to Rob Roy,' he instructed in his normal voice, 'and help him try to get the thing going. Everyone else to scour the town for red and white paint – ten pots of white to one of red. And don't forget the brushes. You'll just have to help yourselves from ironmongers, builders' yards – anywhere. This is an emergency and we'll arrange for compensation afterwards.'

Arthur turned to Drake with a broad grin. 'Sorry, I seem to be doing all the bossing. Sheer force of habit, I'm afraid. Shall we go up to the station and see what state the engine's in? This is all going to take a bit of organizing.'

Drake got up from Freddy's bed, where he had been examining the wounded leg again. 'Right,' he said. 'I suppose "our gallant aeronauts", as you would call them, can look after themselves.'

Together the two eldest boys left the room and hurried downstairs after the others; and a silence, broken only by the murmur of amiable technical conversation between Fritz and Freddy, descended on Adelaide House.

Kemp Town station yard had not seen such activity since it had been closed to passenger traffic eight years before. Gillian and six of the Foulshams, after carrying out a swift and thorough search, arrived singly and in pairs at the station loaded down with pots of paint and brushes; and last of all, beaming with self-esteem, Randolph turned up dragging two long builders' ladders. 'I thought they might come in handy,' he responded in an off-hand voice to Arthur's words of praise for his foresight.

With the sun already low in the sky over the rooftops, they set to work on the shabby old Victorian carriage. There was no question of washing down the chipped and rotting woodwork first; selecting any area at random, they applied the paint with brushes of every size from pots ranging from half-pint to one gallon. Nobody worried about the shade; some of it was deep cream, some near yellow. It was a case of any paint with any brush from any pot, and the fact that a good deal of it was smeared on the windows, clothes, and faces was of no importance.

Perched astride the roof of the carriage, Gillian and Eleanor were sloshing on whitewash with vast distemper brushes, which they occasionally flicked playfully at someone below as they sang at the top of their voices. 'Hey, that's not thick enough – you're only making it grey!' Vincent called out to them. But that did not matter; they could put on three coats quicker than the rest together could apply one.

The work on Rob Roy in the shed was of a more serious kind. Here, by combining their hopelessly inadequate and often contradictory knowledge, Arthur and Jeremy Foulsham, and Drake and Sammy, were attempting to master the intricacies of steam locomotion. Neither Arthur nor Drake had a good mechanical sense, and were working almost from scratch. Sammy's interest in engines had been mostly romantic, so any real practical progress was in Jeremy's hands. It was he who established that there was water in the boiler, and identified the various controls. And by the time the carriage was painted all over (in a wild medley of streaks and blotches of various light shades), the firebox had been cleaned out, and Drake and Arthur were searching the yard with buckets for coal and scraps of wood.

Being enthusiasts for ceremonies, the Foulshams naturally took the lighting of Rob Roy's fire as an excuse for a special celebration. Arthur, perched on the cab roof, made a long speech in praise of the gods of fire and speed, with many references to the glories of the iron road, George Stephenson, and Cornelius Vanderbilt. As he made a sweeping bow to the setting sun, incantations were sung in the packed cab (to which Drake, Gillian, and Sammy contributed, a little self-consciously); and then Jeremy was given the honour of striking and applying the match.

In a hushed silence the f̶...
up, caught the wood and s̶...
gathered strength; a cry of triu̶...
them that the first smoke was es̶...
stack.

'All hail, oh fiery steed, oh fleet co̶...
rails, thou shalt no longer tarry in thy her̶... ...ur
called out. 'And now let's eat, I'm starving.'

Jeremy Foulsham, Drake, and Sammy stayed behind to look after the fire and returned to Lewes Crescent long after dark. They reported that they were confident that they had banked it down satisfactorily for the night, and that they could get steam up quickly in the morning.

'O.K. for a nine o'clock start, Drake?' Arthur suggested over supper in Dr and Mrs Hartford's bedroom, which had now become their headquarters.

'Earlier the better. Sammy found a hand trolley we can use for carrying Freddy. How's the leg feel?' he asked the R.A.F. pilot.

Freddy was as pale as when they had first picked him up, and with his day and a half's growth of beard looked in worse health than ever. But he managed to remain cheerful, and smiled round at the circle of anxious faces suddenly turned towards him. 'Not too bad,' he said. 'How's your head, Fritzy?'

e, fine!' He put aside the empty bowl and
e bow towards Gillian and Eleanor. 'That was a
y nice stew, my dears. It hardly seems possible that it
all came out of tins. I can't expect such an excellent diet
in my prisoner-of-war camp.' Fritz lay down luxuriously
between the linen sheets, unconscious of the curious
attention of all eleven children.

'What do you mean, prisoner-of-war camp?' Sammy
demanded.

'Yes, you might be winning – and then *we'd* all be
prisoners-of-war,' Jeremy Foulsham added. 'Anyway, the
battle has moved away. Listen, you can't hear anything
now.'

It was true. None of them had been aware that the
rumble of battle had died, and none could say when this
silence had taken place.

'I expect they've captured London, then,' Randolph
said cheerfully. 'We'll know tomorrow one way or the
other. We ought to have bets on whether it'll be German
or British soldiers who stop us when we get to the battle
line.'

'Well, I'll tell you one thing,' Sammy announced
indignantly from the end of the German's bed. 'No one's
going to put Fritz in a beastly prisoner-of-war camp.'

'Nor Freddy either,' Jeremy said with equal decision.
And everyone joined in the chorus of outraged protest

that penetrated to every room in Adelaide House, and would have been heard on the other side of Lewes Crescent if there had been anyone to hear.

10

The Meeting on the Viaduct

STERN discipline was called for (and applied by Drake and Arthur) to prevent Rob Roy from being manned by five firemen and four drivers; and it was finally left to Sammy, who hotly claimed to be the only one with footplate experience, to act as driver, with Drake and Jeremy as fireman and assistant.

Sammy contrived to give the impression that Jeremy's instructions were unnecessary, and with studied casualness gently opened the regulator to ease the old shunting locomotive out of its shed.

Rob Roy's behaviour was like that of an old man accustoming himself to the use of his legs after long convalescence. His progress was jerky and unpredictable, his wind unsound, to judge from the distressing grunts and spasmodic hisses that escaped from every joint. But his speed increased with Sammy's growing confidence, and Arthur and two of his brothers managed to move the rusted points only just in time as the engine was reversed back again towards the waiting carriage.

'How are the patients?' Drake called out to Gillian from the footplate.

Gillian and Eleanor, each with a white rabbit under an arm, were helping Fritz up into the compartment reserved for the two wounded men, who were also to be attended (at her strong insistence) by Sybil. 'They're fine,' Gillian called back above the sound of Rob Roy's escaping steam. 'We've got Freddy lying down. He says he *likes* the smell of mice and doesn't mind there being no springs.'

'We're setting Rosemary after the mice if they start being troublesome,' Fritz said cheerfully, holding up the grey rabbit he was carrying for Drake to see before disappearing inside.

'Nonsense, they're vegetarians,' Arthur said, shutting the door on them. 'Come on, all aboard,' he told the last of the Foulshams still scuttling about the rails. 'And no getting out when we stop at any points. O.K., Sammy, let her go!' And he waved a dirty handkerchief to the driver and his firemen and swung on to the guard's step at the rear of the carriage.

The Red Cross train's exit from Kemp Town station was as impressive as it was bizarre. The old 2-2-2 locomotive, a survivor from the days when the Southern was the London, Brighton, and South Coast Railway, was filthy from oil and neglect, as uncertain in its colours as the carriage it was to draw, on which the paint had dried in a patchwork of grey, cream, yellow, and off-white blotches, with the Red Cross on the roof and sides running in scarlet streaks.

At first Sammy's unpractised hand on the regulator sent Rob Roy's driving wheels racing ineffectually on the rails. Then he eased it open more gently, the wheels bit, lost their grip momentarily, bit again, and very slowly they moved forward, to the sound of wild cheers from the open windows of every compartment. They clicked over two sets of points, swung out of the siding on to the main line and headed up the cutting at a growing speed.

Peering through the dirty cab window in a fair imitation of a professional driver's stance, Sammy reached up and pulled the whistle. After hissing uselessly for several seconds, it suddenly emitted an ear-splitting wheezing sound. And it was still screaming out as Rob Roy thrust his way into the tunnel entrance under the houses of Evelyn Road, leaving behind a rising plume of smoke that drifted over the deserted station yard.

When they emerged from the tunnel into the deep cutting on the far side, they were travelling at more than twenty miles an hour, and Rob Roy was panting out his delight at the speed. They crossed the Lewes Road by the high viaduct and swung round towards the main Brighton–Lewes line.

'Ease her up,' Drake told Sammy, but the driver was already shutting off and applying the brakes. He knew every inch of this stretch of permanent way.

Arthur jumped down and ran ahead along the track while the train was still moving. 'It's all right, they're set for us,' he called out, and leapt back on to his step as the carriage came past at an accelerating speed.

Driver Hartford eased over the regulator with the skill born of long experience, and the huge pistons of the crack express drove the vast driving wheels faster and faster. Through the cab window he could see the dead straight track stretching ahead across the Lincolnshire flats . . . if he was to break Mallard's *record-breaking run with his* Silver Bullet, *now was his chance. The wheels beat out the wild rhythm, the wind screamed past the cab as the speedometer crept round past the hundred mark. 110, 115 m.p.h. – the record was within his grasp. A sudden dark blur marked their passage through a tunnel, a station flashed by – and then they were on to the viaduct. . . .*

The Preston viaduct spanned the wide valley on Brighton's northern reaches, a gently curving masterpiece of stone and brick on twenty-seven great arches, linking London Road station with the main London to Brighton line. Below them now were the grey-slated roofs of countless houses stretching far away on each side; there were wide, deserted roads, church spires that thrust up from among the huddled buildings; and far away to the south the blue splash of the sea. The whole town – cold and still, the streets lifeless, the chimneys without smoke – seemed to be spread out beneath them.

Sammy's lips were moving, spelling out the magic figures: *120, 125 miles an hour, 128, 129 – and* Silver Bullet, *in the masterly hands of Driver Hartford, had done it! . . . But what was that ahead? Danger on the line. He could hardly believe his eyes, for coming straight towards them on the same line was an express train. His face taut with urgency, Driver Hartford's hand darted for the emergency brake, and with wheels locked . . .*

Rob Roy shuddered to a halt in the centre of the viaduct.

'Hey, what do you think you're doing?' Drake demanded. 'We don't want to stop here.'

But Sammy, his face set and drained of all colour, ignored his brother's protest, and continued to stare ahead along the track.

'What is it? For goodness' sake, Sammy. . . .' Drake leapt across the coal-strewn footplate and leaned out of the cab behind him, one arm on his shoulder.

Barely three feet separated the buffers of Rob Roy from those of the express locomotive that had halted ahead of them on the same line, a great 4–6–0 monster that towered above the little shunting locomotive, and, but for Sammy's sudden braking, would have hurled them all over the parapet.

'Oh!' exclaimed Drake helplessly. 'Oh – I see. . . . Nice work, Sammy. But what in the name of . . . well, we'll soon see what it's all about. Here they come.'

The driver and his fireman had leapt down from the locomotive's cab and were walking along the narrow path by the viaduct's balustrade: two tough-looking, slightly bewildered railwaymen in blue denim overalls.

'Just what's going on, sonny? That was as near a thing as I've seen in forty years.' The fireman, still holding his shovel, looked up at the three boys standing in mute uncertainty on Rob Roy's footplate. 'Is this a kids' outing or something?'

Drake saw the driver glance incredulously at the coach behind and back again to the cab. He was wiping his hands absentmindedly on a piece of waste, and there was coal dust streaked across his cheeks. 'What d'you make of this, Charlie?' he asked the fireman.

'We've got a couple of injured pilots – we're trying to get them out of Brighton –' Drake said above the sound of hissing steam.

'*Out* of Brighton?' the driver exclaimed. He looked friendlier now, but still too surprised to find a smile. 'Lor' bless you, what're you doing in Brighton? Everyone's been out of Brighton for days, and now it's over we're bringing 'em back again. We're the first lot in. Just dumped a couple of thousand in the station and now we're off back to London – through Lewes so's to keep both main-line tracks open.' He pointed at the old coach and turned to his fireman again. 'Look at that, Charlie – nothing but kids.'

Every door had swung open and the Foulshams were swarming about excitedly over the rails, all shouting at once. 'Look Arthur!' 'Look, another train!' 'Nearly knocked them to blazes!'

'That was a piece of careless driving,' Arthur called out in his deep voice to the driver. 'Might have been a nasty accident. Safety first, that's what I always say. Can't be too careful, you know.' He broke through the crowd and came striding up until he was standing between the fireman and the driver. 'Is the invasion over, or what?' he demanded more seriously.

The driver and fireman had quite recovered themselves and were grinning at Eleanor and Gillian

'Just what's going on?'

who were standing behind Arthur holding their rabbits.

'Got a menagerie, too, eh? Yep, all over,' Charlie told Arthur. 'Haven't you heard? You're about the last then. Sent what was left of 'em back where they came from yesterday. War's not over, of course, but old Hitler's had a nasty shock, I reckon, don't you Jim?'

'Ye-e-es,' agreed the driver, whistling between his teeth. 'Got what was coming, that's what 'e got. But what're we going to do with this lot?'

'Well, there's plenty to look after 'em now,' the fireman said, nodding his head towards the stone balustrade of the viaduct. 'Here they come.'

Drake looked down to the main London road that ran under the viaduct, and saw seventy feet below a motor coach travelling fast towards the centre of the town. Its roof was loaded high with suitcases and grips, prams and bicycles, luggage of all kinds. Another followed it, then another, and a dozen more. Interspersed between them were army trucks packed with the returning refugees, and even a few private cars. One coach had already halted just short of Preston Circus and was disgorging its passengers on to the pavement. Outside one of the big houses in Preston Road, an elderly couple, after being helped out of the back of an army truck by some soldiers, disappeared up their drive.

Brighton was returning to life as rapidly as it had died. The arteries were flowing again, the familiar sound of motors, of tyres on tarmac roads, of voices calling to one another, rose up to Drake's ears . . . and at once the strange feeling of loneliness and of isolation from the familiar world he had always known, slipped away, and became as distant and irrecoverable as a week-old dream. Suddenly, and at a bewildering speed, life was returning to normal.

'Now what's going on here? Just what is this all about?' They all turned at the sound of the high-pitched, carping voice, and identified the stout little figure by his uniform as a senior railway official. 'What are you doing here, boy? Stealing company property, I see, and trespassing.'

Drake's silence and the sight of his expressionless face staring down from the footplate seemed to exasperate the official even further. 'Get down from there, boy, or I'll – I'll see you get a five-year term in Borstal. And you, get down, I say,' he went on, his head bobbing angrily towards Sammy and Jeremy.

When he caught sight of eight more children clustered alongside the coach and eyeing him with a sort of curious malevolence, the little man lost all control. 'What – what – get off my railway. D'you hear me? Get along. I'll have the police on you – the lot of you, I'll –'

And he scurried towards the Foulshams, waving his arms without grace or purpose.

But the Foulshams were experienced hands at frustrating authority. Arthur had dealt with many more difficult officials than this one, and he stood up to him now without any trouble at all. 'Listen, you silly little man,' he told him patiently, resting a hand on his shoulder. 'We're not juvenile delinquents, just get that into your head, will you? In fact if we weren't too modest to say so, we would say we were more like boy scouts doing our good deed of the day – don't you agree all?' he asked the others – and they chorused their agreement: 'Angels, that's us!' 'Look at our haloes!'

The official was rapidly becoming apoplectic, and it was left to Drake to bring some sort of sense to the meeting. 'Look, we've got two wounded men with us,' he told him reasonably, jumping down from the footplate and leading him along to the compartment containing Fritz and Freddy. 'That's why we've painted this old carriage with the Red Cross. You see, we thought the invasion battle was still on. One of these pilots needs medical attention urgently, and we're not leaving them until we know they're in the right hands.'

'It's quite true what they say,' Fritz greeted the man with a smile. 'This wound of mine is nothing,' he said, indicating his bandaged forehead. 'But my friend must have a doctor soon. These children are real heroes and they certainly mustn't get into any trouble on our account.'

'That's right,' Freddy confirmed from his makeshift bed on the seat. 'They deserve a medal, the lot of them.'

The official was now frankly confused, and Drake even began to feel sorry for him. He was the sort of petty bureaucrat who cannot cope with anything that is not of a routine nature, and this was a situation beyond his comprehension. 'Well, I . . .' he began, still attempting to show some aggression.

The engine driver finally settled the matter to everyone's satisfaction. 'Look, how about this, sir,' he said diplomatically. 'Charlie here can take the train on to Lewes, and I'll run Rob Roy out of the way into the sidings, and then take them into Brighton. There'll be plenty of people to look after these wounded men there. Only I think we'd better get the line clear, don't you, sir?' he said, already climbing up into Rob Roy's cab. 'The railway's going to be busy today.'

Still looking bewildered by it all, the official reluctantly agreed. The Foulshams and the Hartfords climbed into the white-painted carriage, and now in more expert hands, Rob Roy was reversed into a siding to allow the express to pass, and then resumed its journey across the viaduct. Slowly and carefully, for the signalling system was not yet fully functioning, Rob Roy was taken across the numerous points and steamed into the station. Their trip had lasted a mere five minutes, and they were all conscious of the sense of anticlimax.

Arthur and Drake were the first to leap down on to the platform before the carriage had halted. The main hall looked as it had on the afternoon of the evacuation, with hundreds of people milling about, clinging on to their luggage and their children. Five long trains were in the platforms, and more people were pouring out of them to join those already in the main hall. Everyone appeared much too concerned with their own problems of searching for lost members of their family or of keeping them together and finding their way back home to be able to help Drake and Arthur. But the boys soon discovered that there was some kind of organization; groups of military policemen were assisting some of the old people, and Drake eventually discovered an ambulance unit on duty near the booking-offices.

The first-aid men accompanied Arthur and Drake back to the carriage, and at once took efficient charge of the situation. 'We'll have to send you two up to London,' Fritz and Freddy were told after an examination. 'We can't cope with this sort of thing. The hospitals here won't be functioning properly for a few days yet. We'll get you on one of the trains right away. They're leaving every few minutes.'

All eleven children were packed in an anxious bunch about the open compartment door when the first-aid men began moving Freddy out on a stretcher. 'Make way there, kiddies,' they were told. 'You've done a good emergency repair job on this leg,' another of the men complimented Drake. 'They say they owe their lives to you, and I can believe it.'

Suddenly Sammy sprang forward and knelt down beside the stretcher held by two of the first-aid men, and whispered something into Freddy's ear.

The R.A.F. pilot replied with a wink. 'That'll be all right, don't you worry, Sammy,' they heard him say quietly. 'I shan't let on, and when they do find out he'll be well looked after. I'll see to that.' He turned to the others. 'Good-bye, and thanks for everything,' he called out.

'Good-bye – good-bye, Fritz. Come and see us when you're better,' they shouted after the retreating figures, which were soon lost in the crowds.

'Well, that's that,' Arthur said. 'All's well that ends well, that's what I always say. And there's another potty platitude for your collection, Eleanor.'

'What were you whispering to Freddy, Sammy?' Gillian asked.

Sammy stood awkwardly on one foot, reluctant to answer. 'Oh, nothing,' he said.

'Come on, let's have it,' they all demanded.

'Well – I was worried about Fritz. You know, talking English like that, I thought they'd think he was a spy when they found out – and maybe shoot him. They do shoot spies, you know,' he said seriously.

'Yes, poor old Fritz,' Arthur said. 'He was right, it will be the prisoner-of-war camp for him. But Freddy's right, too. They won't do him any harm, and they'll look after that wound of his. Drake,' he went on in his more natural and boisterous voice, 'I suppose it's time all horrid Hartfords and foolish Foulshams wended their way homewards – back to orthodoxy and regular habits, back to the dull routine of everyday life. Heigh-ho for the good old days of freedom!'

Drake agreed with a laugh, although he could not help feeling that life for the Foulshams never had been, and probably never would be, dull, orthodox, or regular. 'And poor Sammy never did get his ride on the dodgems, did you?' he said, leading Gillian and his younger brother through the crowds after the Foulshams.

Outside the station, Queen's Road was thick with traffic and the pavements were crowded with hurrying people. Several of the shopkeepers were busy with brooms outside their doors, sweeping the accumulated litter into the gutter. But the proprietor of the newsagent's shop they had passed on that first morning (so many weeks ago now it seemed) had not yet returned, and the damp, dirty newspaper with the headlines 'Invasion Threat Diminishes' was still in its rack.

Everyone they met appeared unusually cheerful, as if, now that they had been suddenly relieved of a great anxiety, they were anxious to tell everyone else how wonderful life was. 'Hullo, nippers, off for a bathe?' a shop assistant cleaning a window called after them. There was an air of busyness and excitement and bustle about the town which they had never before known.

It was like August Bank Holiday in the Old Steine. The sun was out and the coaches pouring in from London, hooting and squeezing their way along the roads, might have been filled with happy excursionists instead of returning refugees. 'Foreigners, nosy intruders!' Arthur grumbled. 'The rats are coming back now they see the ship's not sinking after all. Bah to them all!' For the moment they were all feeling rather low and depressed.

In the gardens a uniformed council official was bending over the fountain control cock, and suddenly after a few preliminary spits, the multitude of jets shot up into the sky to form a tall, delicate pattern of spray.

The official, a tubby character with a walrus moustache, turned away, apparently satisfied.

'Hey, what's this? Can't have this, you know, kiddies,' he said to Gillian and Eleanor when he spotted their rabbits grazing on the grass. 'Can't you read – says Keep Off, don't it? Sorry, but off you go now.'

Even the Palace Pier had lost its magic charm, and appeared as dead as the town had looked only a few hours before. The paintwork on the minarets and cupolas, the decorated railings and the roof of the Palace of Fun, appeared chipped and dirty; and the lights had exhausted the batteries and were now extinguished. Only a few sad-looking toffee apples from the Foulshams' last assault on the armoured car lay about to remind them of earlier, more splendid days. Drake saw a small boy pick one up and suck it reflectively before disappearing behind the Royal Albion Hotel.

All along the Marine Parade people were climbing out of trucks and coaches and taxis and disappearing inside, loaded with trunks and suitcases. Many of the front doors and windows of the houses and hotels were open for the first time for days, and as the Hartfords and Foulshams passed there were cheerful cries of greeting between neighbours. 'Nice to be back, isn't it?' 'Hullo Ethel, dear, how did you get on?' they heard.

Gillian was the first to round the corner into Lewes

Crescent, looking up eagerly towards Adelaide House. But only a few people had arrived back home and the Square was bare of traffic. 'Oh well, I suppose we can at least clear the place up before Mummy and Daddy get back,' Gillian said to Drake, trying to hide her disappointment.

She glanced across the gardens to the far side of the terrace and saw that the front door of the yellow house was wide open. 'George Foulsham's home anyway, and hard at it – look,' she said. 'Eleanor, your father's home,' she called back to the others. 'He's painting on his studio balcony.'

George Foulsham appeared to have heard their voices, for they saw him turn from his easel and give them a perfunctory wave. 'Ah, there you are.' The richly accented voice came to them faintly from across the gardens. 'Thought I hadn't seen you for a few days. Had any adventures?'

'Good old George, he's made it,' Arthur shouted. 'There's no place like home – that's what I always say. Come on, ye fruity Foulshams, let's go and see what the old man's been up to. See you later,' he called to Drake, 'and here's to the next invasion.'

And the eight Foulshams tore away across the gardens, Arthur in the lead and calling 'Tally-ho!', Simon at the rear waving his arms like a windmill's sails and crying out in a high-pitched voice. Only Eleanor paused momentarily in the charge, to put Van Gogh down on the grass for a feed. Then she followed the others, bounding up the front steps four at a time, and disappeared inside.

There was an odd smile on Drake's face as he led Gillian and Sammy up the road towards Adelaide House. Of course it was a daft idea, he was thinking – of course it was impossible to learn anything from that crazy mob, good company though they might be when you had got to know them.

And yet – and yet, Drake decided, perhaps they had learnt something from them after all . . . who knows?

'Drake, look! There they are!' Gillian suddenly exclaimed from beside him.

'And they haven't seen us. Don't call out, let's watch,' Sammy whispered excitedly.

Two figures – one short and dark, the other tall and fair, with her hand tucked into her husband's arm – were walking slowly down the front steps of Adelaide House. They paused beside the armoured car parked outside, and peered first up and then down the road. For one moment of disbelief they were so still they might have been carved in stone.

Then Mrs Hartford broke away and began running, awkwardly in her high heels, with her arms wide and calling out words of greeting that they could not hear.

Gillian led the race towards her, running so fast that first Rosemary and then Kensington leapt from her arms in alarm. . . . But they recovered their composure quite quickly, joined Van Gogh on the lush grass of the gardens, and settled down to a good long feed.

Author's Apology

Although this does not pretend to be a true story, I am sorry if any readers have been left with the false impression that England really was invaded in 1940. It did very nearly happen, of course, and if it had then there is no reason why the adventures I have described could not have taken place; except that, so far as I know, the Palace Pier does not have its own electricity supply, and that during the invasion scare one of its spans was demolished to prevent German invaders from using it. Otherwise the background is authentic.

Perhaps another apology is due to the residents of Brighton – a town in which I was born and grew up, and which I love today – for giving the impression that they would so meekly have allowed themselves to be evicted from their homes.

THE CHILDREN WHO STAYED BEHIND

The Backstory

Find out from Deborah Moggach, the author's daughter, what inspired this wartime tale!

Who's Who in *The Children Who Stayed Behind*

Gillian Hartford: The impulsive middle child. She may appear thoughtless and uncaring but that's far from the truth. She bounces through life like the animals she cares so much about, but when it comes to the pursuit of her beloved rabbit, Kensington, she has the bravery of a warrior, even standing up to the Foulshams.

Drake Hartford: Gillian's older brother, aged fourteen, is rather brainy and can usually be found reading advanced biology, to the despair of Gillian who wishes he could be a bit more fun, like he used to be. He takes the responsibility for his younger siblings when the children are left behind.

Sammy Hartford: The youngest of the Hartford children, aged nine. He used to like trains but now his favourite things are naval history and warships, so he gets very excited when he sees them in Brighton. Because of his obsession he is the first to hear the evacuation order.

Dr Hartford: Father of the three children. He is often so busy working as a doctor that he doesn't get to spend much time with his children. Drake's interest in medicine shows he is following in his father's footsteps.

Mrs Hartford: Mother of the children. She is a bit of a worrier and is nervous about the war and what it will mean for her family. She gets very upset when she is separated from her children at the train station during the evacuation.

Arthur Foulsham: The eldest of the eight Foulsham children. He is a wild-haired ginger terror who is almost six feet tall! As the ringleader of his brothers and sisters, he tries his best to torment the Hartford children as much as possible. Hated by all the Hartfords – though perhaps he isn't as bad as they think.

Eleanor Foulsham: Arthur's sister. She is a bit plump, very freckly and second-in-command of the Foulsham gang. We first meet her when she kidnaps Gillian's rabbit, Kensington, and claims it is her own rabbit, Van Gogh. The chase which follows causes all the children to miss the last train out of Brighton.

Jeremy Foulsham: Another of the Foulsham boys. He is a keen mechanic, which comes in handy when he has to work with Sammy to get the old steam train working again.

Sybil Foulsham: One of the younger sisters. She acts as the nurse of the group and helps bandage the two pilots found on the beach.

Randolph, Vincent, Simon and Rosetti Foulsham: The rest of the Foulsham siblings. All have red hair and love to tease the Hartford kids.

George Foulsham: Father of the eight Foulsham children and a widower. He claims to be a great surrealist painter but he really gets his money from illustrating romantic stories in magazines.

Kensington: Gillian's pet white rabbit. He is kidnapped by the Foulshams and is the cause of various daring rescue attempts. He was bought as a companion to Gillian's other rabbit, Rosemary.

Fritz: The German pilot saved by the children. He uses a convincing English accent to try and hide his nationality, so he's very relieved when the children tell him they will help him out, no matter what.

Freddy: The British pilot also discovered injured with a broken leg after the dog-fight with Fritz. The two pilots learn to put their differences aside while in the care of the children, their rescuers.

Test your knowledge of *The Children Who Stayed Behind*
(Turn to the back for answers – no cheating!)

1) How many children are there in the Foulsham family?
   a) Six
   b) Eight
   c) Ten

2) Why does Sammy's father tell him that he can never become a sailor?
   a) He's too small
   b) He gets seasick
   c) His eyesight is too bad

3) The first time the Hartfords try to get Kensington back, what type of transport do they use?
   a) An armoured car
   b) A helicopter
   c) A bicycle

4) Where do the Foulshams set up camp when Brighton is empty?
   a) West Pier
   b) Main Pier
   c) Palace Pier

CLASSICS

VINTAGE

5) What do the Foulshams attack Drake with when he is on watch?
   a) Cabbages
   b) Rotten toffee apples
   c) Stones

6) What does Eleanor tell Gillian she feeds Kensington?
   a) Candy floss
   b) Carrots
   c) Chicken soup

7) What is the name of the house where the Hartfords live?
   a) Agatha House
   b) Anita House
   c) Adelaide House

8) What is the name of the steam train locomotive the children use to get out of Brighton?
   a) Big Ben
   b) Rob Roy
   c) Loud Larry

9) What is the name of Eleanor's rabbit, which looks very similar to Kensington?
   a) Leonardo

b) Picasso

c) Van Gogh

10) How does Arthur know the first soldier they find on the beach is German?

a) He sees a swastika on his plane

b) From the style of the soldier's moustache

c) He hears him speaking German whilst asleep

Who was Bruce Carter?

Bruce Carter, whose real name was Richard Hough, was born in 1922. He grew up in Brighton, a city he loved his whole life. His father was a bank manager and he had an older sister who sadly died just before he was born. He grew up with a keen interest in the Navy and loved making model warships but one day he discovered that he was seriously seasick, so it's no surprise then, that when the Second World War broke out, he quickly joined the Royal Air Force. He was injured during the war when he shot down two German bombers, causing him to break his leg badly.

After the war was over he had various jobs, including being a delivery driver for a wine shop. He ended up working in publishing, eventually becoming head of a children's book division. However, it wasn't enough just to publish books, so he started writing them too. He wrote books for adults specialising in maritime history and also books for children, like this one, which he wrote using the pen name Bruce Carter.

Writing obviously runs in the family as two of his four daughters are also professional writers. His daughter,

Deborah Moggach, writes novels for adults, and his other daughter, Sarah Garland, writes and illustrates books for children. His granddaughter, Lottie Moggach, is also a novelist.

Bruce Carter died in 1999.

Read on to discover what it was like having a famous author as your father...

A message from Deborah Moggach, the author's daughter

My father, Richard Hough, was born and brought up in Brighton and loved it all his life. In those days children roamed around more freely than they do now and he remembered long days out on his bike, an apple and a lump of cheese in his pocket, only returning home when dusk fell. He particularly loved the seafront – who doesn't? After all, it had slot machines and side-shows and dodgems and candy floss and, best of all, a pier. There's something magical about a pier – a place made entirely for fun, and stretching out so thrillingly into the middle of the sea.

Brighton, like all seaside towns, feels on the edge of the world. The sea is always present – you can smell it and see it, a great infinity, a place of mystery and beauty and adventure. And just across the water lies France, a foreign country – which is the most thrilling thing of all.

My father grew up before the Second World War. When it broke out, in 1939, France was occupied by the Nazis and suddenly became enemy territory. As soon as he was old enough my father joined the Air Force. He became a fighter pilot and made many hazardous journeys across the Channel into France; at the height of the war, the life expectancy for fighter pilots was just nineteen days!

Luckily he survived or you wouldn't be reading this book. Though England wasn't invaded, thank goodness, he always had a vivid imagination. Like all writers he constantly asked himself 'What if?...' which is the way all stories begin. In this case it was 'What if England was invaded?' What if the town was evacuated and all that was left were some children – who, as you know, have a much more interesting time when there are no adults around.

My father started writing for children when my sisters and I were young. He worked at home, tapping away on a typewriter in our cramped little cottage just outside London. He showed us his stories when they were still loose sheets of paper, and asked our reactions. I loved this; it made me feel grown-up, with an opinion that was valued, and this is so important for a child. It also made writing stories seem the most natural thing in the world (and indeed, I grew up to be a novelist).

My father drew on our lives quite a bit; we'd recognize things we'd said or done in his books. In this story, however, he also drew on his own childhood in the town he loved – a town whose existence was so nearly threatened by war.

But there were things from our childhood, too, in the book. One thing in particular. When it was first published, the book was called *The Kidnapping of Kensington*. We always had a lot of animals, especially rabbits (which we considered, quite rightly, more interesting than guinea pigs). Around this time my sister, Sarah, had a big white rabbit called Kensington. He was absolutely gorgeous. She used to carry him around everywhere and I can still remember the stab of envy when I saw him in her arms. Like all our rabbits he was very tame, hopping around the house like one of the family.

And, such is the magic of fiction, he's not been forgotten. He still lives on, a living breathing rabbit, the hero of his own story. Or was he a she? I honestly can't remember. But that's part of the story too.

My father wrote many books but this is my favourite. I do hope you enjoy it too.

Are you a rabbit owner? Or do you aspire to have a furry friend? If so, here's a handy fact-sheet on rabbits...

Things rabbits like

Food: Gillian is horrified by Eleanor's claim that she has been feeding Kensington candy floss, and quite right too. Rabbits mostly eat hay and grass but love the occasional fruit or vegetable too.

Hopping: Rabbits love to get lots of exercise and, in fact, they need as much exercise as small dogs! That is why it's important for them to have a big space to explore and a roomy hutch so that they can hop freely.

The floor: As rabbits are preyed upon in the wild they much prefer to have all four paws on the floor, so they can scurry away in moments of danger. Picking rabbits up is not their preferred thing; they prefer it when humans come down to floor level to play.

Friends: In the wild, rabbits live in large groups and so, as pets, they like to have other rabbit companions around them. They can get very lonely if they have no friends.

That's why Gillian is keen to get Kensington, as a friend for her grey rabbit, Rosemary.

Hiding places: As rabbits like to hide themselves away if they sense a predator, such as a dog, cat or fox, it's important to give them lots of straw to burrow into. They also love cardboard boxes with a small hole cut in the side. The reason rabbits have eyes on the side of their heads is so they can easily look out for predators. The reason they have such long ears is so they can hear approaching predators. The reason they have lovely twitchy noses is because they're always smelling things and checking for the whiff of predators.

Digging: Because in the wild they live in burrows, rabbits love to have a good dig. Give them a sandpit, a flower-bed or a box filled with shredded paper and they will have a whale of a time.

Things rabbits don't like

Guinea pigs: Although it's quite common to keep rabbits and guinea pigs together, it's not a good idea to make them live together all the time. It's not that they have anything against each other, but just because they are different species of animal, so they can't understand one another.

Also, rabbits have strong back legs – if they kick out and a guinea pig is in the way it can cause serious injury to the poor old guinea.

Ear holding: Although it's the traditional way for magicians to pluck white rabbits out of top hats, rabbits hate to be picked up by the ears. I mean, would you like it?

Hot days: A rabbit's favourite times of day are dawn and dusk. Because they have a lot of fur they tend to lounge around during hot days and get more active when it becomes cooler.

Grass cuttings: Although rabbits love grass, they like to nibble it fresh from the lawn. Feeding them lawn-mower cuttings can make them ill. Eleanor Foulsham might have done Kensington a favour when she flung the bag of cut grass into the sea.

Water: Rather like cats, rabbits hate to be bathed. Fortunately there's no need to put them through the ordeal of bath time as rabbits are very good at cleaning themselves by licking.

Have a look at http://www.rspca.org.uk/adviceandwelfare/pets/rabbits for more info on keeping rabbits.

The Second World War – the facts

Although you can just imagine the events depicted in *The Children Who Stayed Behind* really happening, they were of course made up by the author. German troops never arrived on British soil. But the Second World War really did happen and it had very real effects for adults and children all over Britain. Here are a few ways in which the war affected children around the country.

Rationing

During the war, the government was worried there wouldn't be enough food to go around. Ships carrying imports of food would sometimes be blown up and the armed forces required huge quantities of food. For that reason they decided to limit the amount each person could consume. This was rationing.

The first foods to be rationed in 1940 were bacon and other types of meat, sugar, tea and butter. In 1941 eggs were rationed – you were allowed just one egg each week. Later on, other things were rationed, including sweets, clothes and soap.

Some products were not rationed but became very tricky to get hold of. Lemons and bananas almost disappeared from Britain during the war. Many younger children did not see a banana in real life until after the war ended. Some even doubted their existence!

However, people were encouraged to grow their own fruit and veg and lots of children helped out in gardens and allotments around the country. The government had a campaign which called on people to 'Dig for Victory', so lots of children helped to do exactly that. It was a way for young people to help the war effort at home.

Evacuation

When war broke out it was clear that German bombers would target cities, where all the factories were located. To keep them out of harm's way, many city children were sent to live in the countryside, away from their parents. This was called evacuation.

Some children were able to go and stay with relatives or friends in the country, but many had to go and stay with strangers. Often they would line up and people would pick which children they wanted to take home. Although about

800,000 kids were sent away, quite a lot returned within a few weeks.

The Blitz

Enemy planes performed air raids in which they dropped bombs on British cities. They dropped big bombs that landed with great explosions that tore down buildings and smaller bombs, called incendiaries, that started fires.

The Blitz is the name given for a series of air raids that started in September 1940. Many major cities and ports were targeted including London, Birmingham, Coventry, Southampton, Sheffield, Manchester, Liverpool, Hull and Glasgow.

When enemy planes approached, an air-raid siren would be sounded to warn everyone to get to a safe place. Some people had built special shelters in their gardens out of corrugated iron called Anderson shelters. There were also public shelters. In London many people went down into Underground train stations. They would stay in the shelter for as long as the sirens were signalling, often sleeping there in uncomfortable conditions.

Education

Children still had to go to school right through the war, and evacuees went to new schools near their new homes. Alongside regular lessons like maths and English, children also learned about what to do in air raids. If an air-raid siren sounded when they were at school, everyone would go to a shelter together, carrying their gas masks, until the raid had passed.

Playtime

Many of the factories and materials for making toys and games had to be used for weapons and other war equipment, so there weren't many new toys around. Children would swap old toys and play in the street – sometimes in the wreckages of bombed-out buildings – and with games made of paper or card. Not many people had TVs back then; instead children listened to the radio or to records played on a gramophone. The cinema showed films, cartoons and news programmes.

Family life

Many family homes in the 1940s were less comfortable than ones today. Some did not have a toilet – you had to go to an outside loo – and baths were made of tin and set in front of the fireplace. Because of water rationing people would have to share their bathwater with the whole family. People had to use blackout curtains to stop any lights showing at night, so enemy bombers would find it hard to spot cities from the air. They also put paper tape across the windows so that if a bomb exploded nearby it wouldn't blow in the window, sending sharp bits of glass all through the house.

Telephones often didn't work, because of the bombing, so people would send messages by posting letters. Another way of communicating was by telegram.

For many children in wartime their dads, uncles and older brothers went off to fight whilst mums, aunts and older sisters had to find work in the factories. It was a very unsettling and dangerous time for everyone. More than 60,000 people in Britain died in the bombing raids. Factories, schools and homes were destroyed.

Answers to *The Children Who Stayed Behind* quiz – how did you do?

1) b – Eight

2) c – His eyesight is too bad

3) a – An armoured car

4) c – Palace Pier

5) b – Rotten toffee apples

6) a – Candy floss

7) c – Adelaide House

8) b – Rob Roy

9) c – Van Gogh

10) a – He sees a swastika on his plane

VINTAGE CLASSICS

Visit **www.worldofstories.co.uk**